BOOKS BY C.B. WILSON

Jack Russelled to Death
Cavaliered to Death
Bichoned to Death
Shepherded to Death
Doodled to Death
Corgied to Death
Aussied to Death
Dachshund to Death
Labradored to Death
Puppied to Death
Retrievered to Death (Coming 2025)

PRAISE FOR BARKVIEW MYSTERIES

See what readers are saying about Barkview Mysteries in these five-star reviews:

"If you are looking for a mystery to tax your clue-connecting skills then Doodled to Death is one novel you should read. Its quirky humor and intelligent banter give it the feel of a Nancy Drew and Miss Marple murder mysteries hybrid with an even more exciting conclusion."
—Reader's Favorite, 5-star review

"I couldn't put the book down! The writing is top-caliber, the characterization three-dimensional, the concept clever, and the plot is compelling. (Not to mention the cute, opinionated dogs…) This cozy mystery will enthrall both dog lovers and history lovers."
—Lori H, Amazon

"CB Wilson is a fun, fresh voice on the cozy mystery scene."
—Sherri I., Amazon

"C. B. Wilson has done it again. Her cozy mysteries are full of charisma, they are entertaining, full of life, and very descriptive! Every one I read captivates me until the very last page. Love these books!!"
—babygirl, Amazon

"Fast-paced, well-written and clever mystery that will tickle the fancy of dog lovers and non-dog lovers alike."
—BH, Amazon

BICHONED TO DEATH

A BARKVIEW MYSTERY

C. B. WILSON

CONTENTS

To Brandi & Bailey
Love you both

1. Bow Wow Boutique
2. Posh Puppies
3. Bichon Bisquet
4. Beg-als Shoppe
5. Muttropolis
6. Woofing Best Coffe
7. Urban Pup
8. Snooty Pooch
9. Fluff & Buff
10. Fiesta Chihuahua
11. Bank
12. Gem's Palace
13. Blooming Tails
14. Taj Ma Hound
15. Hot Dog Stand
16. Bone Garden Salad
17. Attorney
18. Escrow
19. Hair Salon
DOG PATH
Cat's Town House
2nd
3rd
4th
Homes
1st
K9 Fine Wine Bar
Graveyard & Ghost
Hounds Hardware
Frosty Pup
Chateau Chienn
Salty Dog Seafood
Doodle Pad
KDOG Studio
Mutt Hutt
Dogwo
Farmer's Market
Dolce
Ciao Bella
Dog House
A Lifeguard Tower
B
A
B Old Barkview Inn
WOOF
DOG PATH

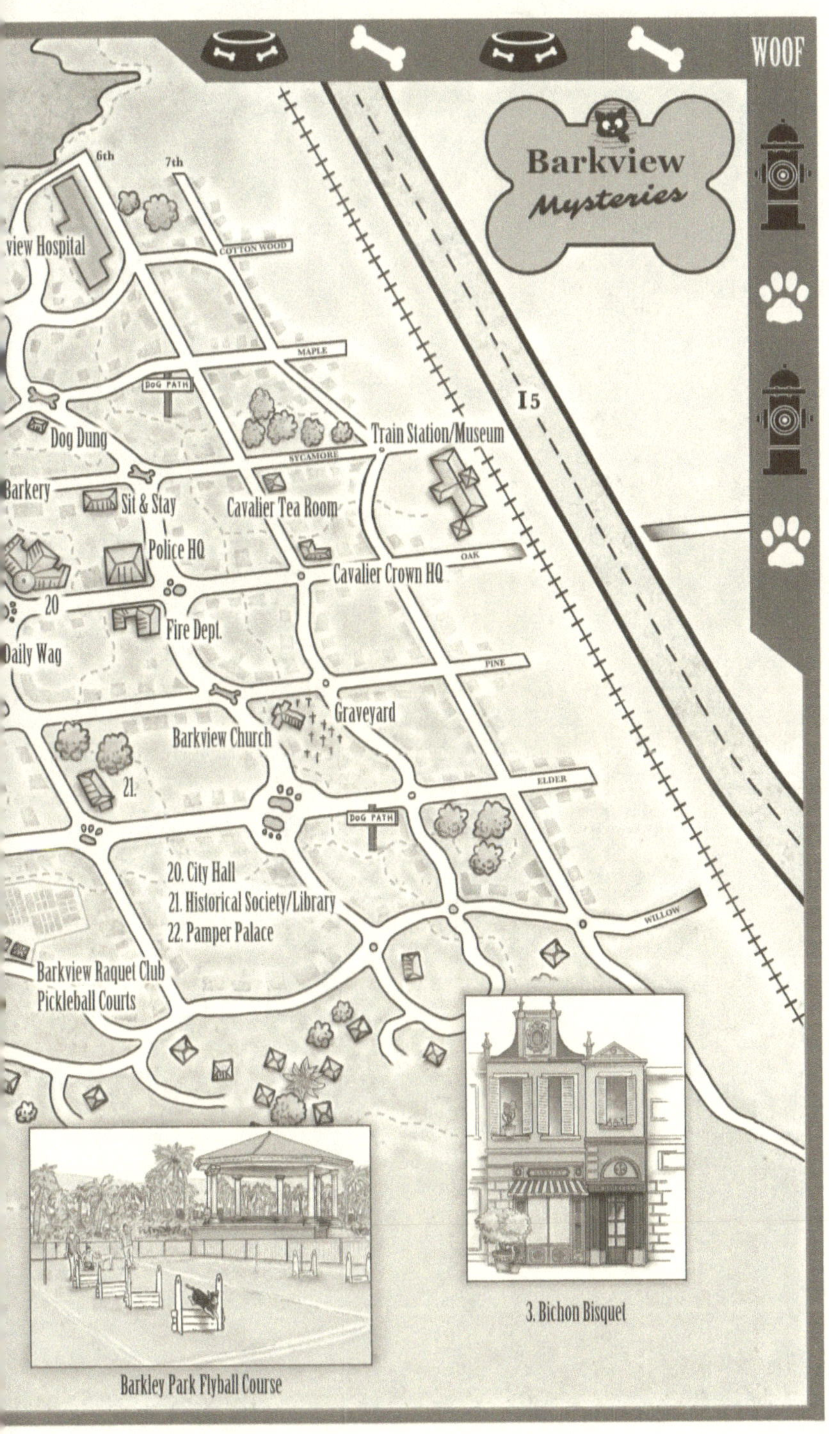

Barkley Park Flyball Course

3. Bichon Bisquet

CHARACTERS HUMAN

Barklay, Celeste: Founder Barkview in 1890

Barklay, Charlotte (Aunt Char): Owner champion Cavalier King

Charles, Renny. Dog Psychiatrist on *Throw Him a Bone*.

Barklay, JB: Charlotte's late husband

Collins, Roland and Brooke: Barkview's trash czar

Conti, Giuseppe: friend of Grandpa Principato (Tina Looc's grandfather and Angela's father)

Daniels, Jimmy: owner Barkage Garage. JD Junkyard, part–Pit Bull, part–something else, is his dog

Duncan, Franklin: concierge at the Old Barkview Inn

Fountaine, Rayelle: owner of Bichon Bisquets, dog bakery. Chef on *Fido's Food Fest*. Cat's sorority sister

Hawl, Russ: FBI consultant. Works for Blue Diamond Security

Hernandez, Marcos Ramirez III: Joey's friend with diabetes

Le Fleur, Michelle: owns Fluff and Buff Salon. Fifi, a black standard Poodle, is her dog

Looc, Howard: Rayelle calls him Ward. Estranged wife Tina. Children Joey and Bianca. Owns Petronics. Bolt, a Border Collie is his dog

Looc, Joey and Bianca: Tina and Howard's diabetic son and daughter

Looc, Tina Principato: owns Ciao Bella Dolce, a competing barkery. Howard's estranged wife. Bella, a Spinone Italiano, is her dog

McCarthy, Stephanie and Stephan: twin brother and sister, co-owners of Frosty Pups Creamery and Graveyards and Ghosts tours. BB, a Blue Bay German Shepherd, is Stephanie's dog

Mel and Nell: sister owners of BIS Barkery and Sit and Stay Café. Brisbane, an Australian Shepherd is Mel's dog. Blur, a black lab, is Nell's dog

Oldeman, Will: elevator operator at the Old Barkview Inn

Papas, Ariana and Chris: owners of Gem's Palace Jewelry. Gem, a German Shepherd, is their dog

Principato, Angela: Tina's mother

Principato, Joseph: Tina's late father and Angela's husband

Principato, Nonna: Tina's grandmother

Richards, Richie: police officer

Riley, Sean: J. Tracker's president. JRu, a Jack Russell Terrier, is his dog

Russo, Jen: Moxie, a Border Collie on Howard's flyball team, is her dog

Sandy: Cat's assistant and computer wiz. Jack, a Jack Russell Terrier, is her dog

Schmidt, Gregory (Uncle G): Barkview's police chief. Max and Maxine, silver-point German Shepherds, are his dogs

Thorpe, Alan: Petronics general manager and CFO. Hawn, a Golden Retriever on Howard's flyball team, is his dog

Thorpe, Tiffany: Alan's daughter

Tuner, Gabby: owner of Daily Wag coffee shop. Sal, a Saluki, is her dog

Wilton, Mark: KDOG's lawyer

Wright, Catalina "Cat": Producer/investigative reporter at KDOG. A cat person living in Barkview

CHARACTERS CANINE

🐾BB: Stephanie McCarthy's Blue Bay Shepherd

🐾Bayle: Rayelle Fontaine's Bichon Frise

🐾Bella: Tina Looc's Spinone Italiano

🐾Bolt: Howard Looc's Border Collie

🐾Brisbane: Mel's red Australian Shepherd

🐾Blur: Nell's black Labrador Retriever

🐾Fifi: Michelle Le Fleur's black standard Poodle

🐾Gem: Ariana and Chris's tan-and-black female German Shepherd

🐾Hawn: Alan Thorpe's Golden Retriever; daughter of Golden (Alan's first Flyball champion dog)

Jack: Sandy's Jack Russell Terrier

JD Junkyard: Jimmy Daniels's dog

Matata: Russ's mother's Portuguese Water Dog

Moxie, a Border Collie

Renny: Aunt Char's champion Cavalier King Charles Spaniel

Sal: Gabby Turner's Saluki dog

CHAPTER 1

I really stepped into it this time. Not a puny poo either, but a super-pooper pile while wearing my favorite strappy sandals. Is it any wonder I prefer sleek, independent, and litter box–trained cats?

My name is Catalina Wright, Cat to my friends. After I'd nabbed the Cavalier dognapper a few months ago, you'd think Barkview would've welcomed me to the pack. I'd even put this town on the national radar by creating and producing the cable sensation *Fido's Food Fest*, cheffed by Bichon Frise owner Rayelle Fountaine.

Brilliant concept, catastrophic execution. Clearly, I'd broken some Canine Commandment. Why else would someone prank Rayelle's recently-opened Barkery, Bichon Bisquets? In the dog-friendliest city in America, a talented, dog-loving chef should've fit right in. Not so much, it turns out. Who knew even Mayberry viewed competition as grounds for a dogfight?

And talk about bold. Not only were Rayelle and I right inside the glass storefront, but three members of my production team had filed out that same door less than twenty minutes prior after filming next week's "Three-Ingredient Biscuits" episode. In this no-secrets town, someone knew something. The trick was finding the right person. I'd get on that, but first the warm goo oozing between my toes needed attention.

I must've screamed bloody murder because Rayelle charged out the glass door, her chef's knife ninja-ready. Bayle, her cotton-ball Bichon Frise, stood at her heels, barking with Doberman fervor.

"Cat! Are you...?" Rayelle's situation assessment took a split second. "Aw, yuck." Empathy zero, I realized, when Rayelle's chuckle exploded into a tear-inducing howl. She tucked her knife into a leather sheath at her waist. Dressed in a white chef's jacket and an eye-matching sky-blue, Bichon-printed apron tied around an enviably trim waist, she looked far too put-together to have just filmed a cooking show with a Bichon helper.

"You gotta watch where you step." Rayelle pinky-wiped away tears.

As if anyone would expect a poo pile on the doorstep. I shot her the evil eye. "Not funny."

"You know, there's a saying around dogs. There are those who have stepped in it and those who will."

"And I thought pick-up-after-your-dog laws served a purpose." Violate that one in Barkview and the national debt seemed surmountable. I should know. I'd challenged every dog-related ordinance during my ten years here.

"When you have 1.2 dogs per resident, hound playgrounds at every roundabout, and designated leash lanes, I'd lay odds it happens often."

No doubt. "You wouldn't think it's so funny if you'd stepped in it in your new Jimmy Choos."

Rayelle's nose crinkled in agreement. Although short by most standards, her stiletto fetish gave her statuesque status. "I usually go out the back way. It's easier to lock up." Like many downtown store owners, Rayelle lived in an apartment above her shop.

"You mean it was meant for me?"

"Stop being paranoid. It's probably just another prank." Rayelle held open the door. "Unless you want me to hose you off, you'd better come in."

As if I had a choice. Unwilling to track crap across the pristine black-and-white-tiled floor, I hopped back inside. Café tables covered with light-blue Bichon-printed tablecloths and Halloween baby-boo pumpkin centerpieces with scroll backed chairs offered the most direct route to the backroom sink.

I nudged Bayle from beneath with my doo-dooed foot. Other than allowing an occasional butt scratch, the dog rarely came within a few feet of me. In fact, when he wasn't glued to Rayelle's side, he chased a miniature tennis ball launched from a boxy contraption behind the retail counter. Even now, a slobbery red ball filled in for a tongue while a small chef's hat drooped over his right ear.

"Ugh! What is it you see in that dog?" He tested my zero tolerance for misbehaving dogs the way he ran figure eights through my legs with circus-clown precision, daring me not to smile. "Don't you dare say cuteness."

"Cuteness is a given. Truth is, he makes me laugh."

I really had to wonder about her sense of humor.

"My aunt owned Bayle's grandsire. That dog was hilarious." Rayelle prodded him aside and slid her shoulder beneath my arm. "Let me help you. I wouldn't take this"—she motioned to my foot—"personally."

She had to be kidding. "Someone is going to pay."

The battle for political correctness waged in Rayelle's expression. "Good luck with that," she said finally.

Ugh! When was enough enough already? I'd reported the toilet-papered front window last week and the birdseed piled on the outdoor tables to the police chief who hadn't even attempted to hide his amusement. Was I the only one lacking a sense of humor regarding vandalism?

"Relax. Remember our college sorority pledge days?" Rayelle asked.

How could I forget? Laughter had gotten us through our first quarter mishaps together and forged a sisters-forever friendship.

"News flash. Hazing is not acceptable," I insisted.

Rayelle's arched brow said otherwise. "You can't fix this for me. I need to pay my dues. I know it and so do you." She guided me to the stainless steel utility sink and turned on the water. Suds grew in the tub while she dragged over a counter stool. I hopped up and dangled my foot over the basin. Rayelle put on gloves.

"Your shoes are...maybe not ruined." Rayelle sniffed. "Could be worse. It doesn't stink too badly."

True. In fact, it kind of smelled like the butcher shop. Regardless, the warm goo oozing between my toes still demanded immediate retribution. I even had the makings of a plan until Rayelle's amusement turned to red-hot anger. "Omg! That's not dog feces. It's pâté."

"Fois gras"—Chateau Chien's trendy version with freshly torn bread and a bottle of Bordeaux came to mind—"looks like dog crap?" Maybe it kind of did.

Bayle jumped into my lap and licked my toes in total agreement. If something smashed between my toes wasn't weird enough, just add warm tongue slobber. Good thing I didn't jerk away. We'd have lost that fluff-ball in the suds for sure. "In the scheme of things, this isn't too bad." This prankster still had way too much time on his or her hands.

"Hardly." Rayelle shooed the dog away and rinsed my foot with warm spray. "Whoever did this wanted an animal convention on my doorstep."

"Huh?" I tucked a tawny hair strand into my no-nonsense ponytail and righted an animal-print scarf.

"Wild coyotes or skunks..."

"Barkview isn't on the outskirts of civilization." Except for my shoes, this could've been far worse. "It's a statement though."

Of the three competing Barkview barkery owners, this stunt seemed very Tina Loocish. Her very public argument with her now-estranged husband, Howard, on *The Bark View*, KDOG's all things Barkview morning show, had been hauntingly similar.

"I had cameras installed this afternoon in the front of the store. I'll finish the online setup tonight," Rayelle informed me.

My gaze followed hers to the Bichon-face wall clock. "It's almost nine. I'll help you in the morning." Actually, I'd call my assistant, Sandy, to help. Syncing my phone to my wireless headphones tested my techy know-how. Sandy, on the other hand, had all things to do with computers wired.

"Nine already?" She attacked the mess on my toes with a diligence I wished my pedicurist exhibited.

"Geez. Got a hot date or something?" I asked.

Her flush had to be from exertion and the steaming water, right? "You want it all off, don't you?"

"Yeah, but I'd like to keep my toes."

"Wimp." Her scrubbing intensity lessened, but not the speed.

"Any idea who did this?" I asked.

"The Frosty Pups Creamery owners are pretty cold to me."

Hardly news there. The black Irish sister-and-brother duo generally socialized with the beach set. "You did ice their Pups Cream on your show last week." Granted, dog ice cream made no sense to me, but what did I know about a pooch's summer treat preferences?

"You know how I feel about gimmicks that don't benefit a dog's health," Rayelle said.

"They and half the county tuning in to your show know how you feel." More importantly, all of Barkview did, too. "You gave a great review to BIS Barkery's breed-specific treats."

"Well, it's a good idea to add beneficial supplements to meet a dog's health needs."

Nell, our number one Oak Street lunch spot owner, and her sister, Mel, also owned Best Ingredients Snacks Barkery, BIS for short. While I considered Nell a friend, subtlety didn't exactly fit her sister's personality.

"Okay. Clean." Rayelle tossed me a towel and dunked my fabric-top sandal into the soapy water. "This is going to take some soaking. I'd better keep these until tomorrow." She yawned, settling off a chain reaction that included Bayle.

Did I imagine another furtive look at the clock? "I can clean them."

"Don't argue. My shoes won't fit you, but my slippers will. Here." Rayelle reached into her I HEART BICHONS backpack and removed fuzzy Bichon heads with treads.

Great. Not exactly in sync with my jungle-cat style. "Uh, I don't think…"

"You want to chance it out there barefoot?"

I slipped my toes into the toasty-warm slippers. Ugh! Just call me a carnival sideshow. Who else dressed in a leopard-print blouse and dark slacks with powder puffs for feet? "If you tell anyone, I'll have to kill you."

"Who'd believe me anyway?"

Fact or fiction didn't slow down Barkview's gossipmongers one bit. "I'll take a look outside for clues."

"No! I mean, it's okay. The cameras will solve the mystery tomorrow night." Rayelle yawned even less subtly. "It's been a long day."

Granted she'd worked the Sunday barkery crowd and then filmed for three hours, yet I felt like I'd just been dismissed. I glanced at the fluffy slippers and shook my head. I wasn't exactly on my game either.

I even convinced myself I'd imagined everything on the drive home. The typical dense marine layer cloaked the ocean-front drive in an eerie mist that allowed only ghostly halos to hover above the turn-of-the-century gas streetlights. Except for the occasional parked car, I had the road to myself.

I kicked off the slippers before the garage door closed, yet the unease followed me. Something was going to happen—something I wasn't going to like. Don't ask me how I knew it. My churning gut just did.

I ignored the call-to-action for over an hour before I gave in and dialed Rayelle's number. No real surprise, the call went straight to voice mail. Concern? I wasn't sure yet.

I dumped what remained of my shiraz-du-jour down the drain, changed into dark jeans and an even darker sweatshirt, ran a brush through my in-need-of-a-trim mane, and climbed into my Jag SUV in eleven minutes flat. Too many scruffy encounters with Russ Hawl, the seriously handsome FBI consultant who'd helped me catch the Cavalier dognappers, had taught me real respect for my Aunt Char's always-be-prepared mantra. I never left home without lipstick and a touch of blush anymore. Almost never.

My garage door closed as my grandfather clock chimed twelve. I dialed 911, but stopped short of connecting the call. Dispatch would wake the police chief right away. Was I ready for a yawn-inducing lecture on a hunch? Better to postpone that confrontation until I had something to tell.

I called Sandy, my KDOG production assistant and contact with generation millennial, as I drove south through the wispy First Street fog.

Sandy answered on the second ring. "Yeah, Boss. What's up? Did we forget anything?" Her unending perkiness should get on my nerves. Not tonight.

"Don't you ever sleep?" During our sixteen months' acquaintance, I don't remember catching her even yawning.

"I own a Jack Russell."

Question answered. "Sorry to bother you this late, but I have a feeling..."

"Not again."

My thoughts verbalized.

"What do you need me to do?" No hesitation. I liked that about her.

"Meet me at Bichon Bisquets."

"Rayelle caught her prankster?" A question or a statement? I wasn't sure.

"I don't know. I'll be there in five minutes." But deep down I did know and it wasn't good.

I turned on to Maple Street expecting...something. Not the majestic Victorians proudly dwarfing the gas lamps and any-day-Barkview quiet broken only by whistling ocean breezes and a distant howl. I U-turned at the Third Street roundabout and parked right in front of the Bichon-shaped Bisquets sign. Except for the faint bluish glow behind the retail counter, the shop's expansive bay windows remained inky dark. The neon CLOSED sign said it all. I had lost my mind. Nothing looked unusual.

I reached into my glove compartment and grasped my go-to six-inch, heavy-duty flashlight anyway. Brandishing it like a weapon, I tiptoed to the front door. Dressed in cat-burglar black, I looked like anything but a concerned citizen. It would be just my luck to get hit with an attempted B&E or malicious mischief charge after I'd reported the not-so-cute pranks going on.

I noticed a green light glowing on the new security camera above the entry right away. Naturally, Rayelle had activated it. Now, I'd be on film stalking the place. I cupped my eyes and peered into the building. Nothing...wait. Was it a shadow or was something slumped in the chair in the far corner? I pointed my flashlight toward the shape.

Suddenly, glass shattered followed by a heart stopping, out-for-blood growl. My scream jammed in my throat as white bicuspids leaped right out of the shadows!

Instinctively, my arms crossed, protecting my face as something plowed into my chest. I fell backward, my shoulder hitting the concrete with a thud. Next thing I knew, two paws pressed my chest down while black eyes glared right into mine.

This was no intent-to-kill Pit Bull. I spat the dog's long, white hairs out of my mouth. A Border Collie? A silver license swinging hypnotically from side to side confirmed everything. What was Howard Looc's dog doing outside Bichon Bisquets? More importantly, why was this normally docile family dog behaving so aggressively?

CHAPTER 2

"I can't wait to hear this explanation." Relief replaced fear the moment I recognized the Chief of Police's voice. Bolt did too. Although the dog's snarls changed to growls, his furtive looks toward the shop did not stop.

"Will you get this dog off me?"

"Bolt, heel." The Border Collie obeyed on command. Uncle G's gotcha radar had certainly found its target tonight. I couldn't even blame it on some DNA connection since the police chief was my Aunt Char's second husband's brother-in-law. I grimaced as I rolled onto my right side, surprised at how my shoulder stuck to the pavement. My elbow would feel this evening's adventure twofold on the pickleball court in the morning.

I stood, flanked by Max and Maxine, Uncle G's two at-attention, silver-point German Shepherds. The police chief epitomized my theory that people chose canine look-alikes. The dog's silvery-gray coats matched Uncle G's neatly clipped Santa Claus beard and hair.

I ignored the dogs, instead focusing on the chief's right-off-the-hanger pressed uniform. "You haven't worked the night shift in a decade. Why are you here?" I asked.

"Got a report of a dog howling in a car in the alley between Third and Fourth Streets." His nonchalant tone didn't fool me. The bobbing toothpick between his lips conveyed his concern.

"Protecting Howard Looc again, I see." I bit my tongue too late. The accusation just slipped out. Although information about Howard's questionable ethics had come to my attention during the Cavalier investigation, Uncle G had not pursued it.

The chief's toothpick snapped. "What's going on here, Cat?"

The secrets continued. I yoga-breathed. "You wouldn't believe me if I told you." I hated that try-me brow lift, the one that cowered even seasoned police officers. "Fine. I had a feeling something was wrong here."

"And you didn't think to call me?"

"At this hour? No one wakes you without a defendable cause." His cuss startled me. Served him right for being so inflexible. "My call to Rayelle went right to voicemail." I shone my flashlight at the counter. "See that shape near the cash register? Does it look like just a shadow?"

The LED beam from his Tactical Pro flashlight joined mine. The glass refraction offered no additional definition. With his free hand he pressed the shop's intercom.

Bayle barked a moment before a light flicked on upstairs. Rayelle's groggy voice came through the voice box. "W-what did they do now, Chief?"

"We need to talk now," Uncle G said.

"Uh, hold on. Bayle, quiet." The barking ceased. "It's after midnight."

"It is." Firm and unyielding, his military police persona worked every time.

"Give me a minute," Rayelle said.

"Open the downstairs door."

Bolt's whining and pawing at the glass door nearly drowned out the buzz. The moment the door clicked open the dog darted inside, his barking frenzied. Not to be left out, Max and Maxine followed. Uncle G sprinted after them. A sweet metallic odor hit me as I paused in the entry, feeling along the raised lattice decor for the light switch. I flipped the switch at the exact moment Uncle G yelled, "Don't look, Cat. You don't want to see this."

Too late. I saw it all. Man, did I ever wish I'd let that sleeping dog lie. Howard Looc slumped forward in the delicate café chair, his arms hanging at his sides, his face planted on the table with a knife sticking right out of his upper back. Not any old knife, but Rayelle's white-handled knife with the Bichon carved into the hilt. "Is...is he d—?" I tasted bile.

"Don't you dare throw up in here," Uncle G snapped.

Maxine's growl stunned me straight out the door I'd just entered. Too bad I tripped over Bayle and stumbled into Rayelle as she entered the front door. Otherwise, I could've protected her. In the end, she had an eagle's view over my shoulder. My ears rang with her screams.

At Uncle G's command, Maxine herded us outside. We braced our backs against the gingerbread-shingled building and sucked in big gulps of air, glad for the long shadows behind the saucy, bereted scarecrow presiding over the purple lilac urn separating the main barkery entrance from Rayelle's quarters. I couldn't get Howard's zombie-like look out of my mind or that nasty, now-definitive smell out of my nose. Eventually, Rayelle's repetitive *Omg, Omg* broke through my brain chaos. Ever-poised Rayelle worse in a crisis than me? I squeezed her hand in solidarity.

The sirens sounded mere blocks away when Sandy arrived. "Geez. You both look like something the cat dragged in." I choked on her euphemism. Trust Sandy to alleviate the tension with bad humor. As usual, she looked model perfect, even dressed in a zip-front Bark U sweatshirt and leggings that emphasized her forever legs with her long blonde hair pulled back in a low ponytail.

"Howard Looc is dead." I didn't wait for her reaction. We had about two minutes before the emergency vehicles arrived and the police sealed off the area. Not to mention the arrival of our Barkview looky-loos. Already, a light shone in every above-store window on the block.

Tomorrow morning's headline, "Bichoned to Death," came to mind.

Entrepreneur Howard Looc murdered at the new Bichon
Bisquets Barkery with Chef Rayelle's signature Bichon knife

The same knife she'd used with an acrobatic flare on nationwide TV just last week.

Clarity struck. My gut felt like I'd been sucker punched by a heavyweight. Like it or not, my star chef and sorority sister was dead center in a murder investigation.

"Sandy, please leave the camera here and check around the corner in the alley behind the Fluff and Buff. See if Howard's car is parked..."

"It is." I hardly recognized that squeak as Rayelle's richly seductive voice. "I was the last person to see him alive."

That bombshell took a moment to process. The sirens almost upon us jolted me to action. Before the situation esca-lated further, I needed to see the surveillance footage. I waved Maxine aside and rose, wiping whatever I'd gotten on my hands from the ground on my pants. Rayelle scooped Bayle into her arms as she ushered me and Sandy upstairs.

I saw the cotton-candy-pink blotches on his front paws the moment we entered the apartment where the barkery's Parisian flair minus the fall decorations continued. Cheery yellows and bright cornflower blues graced the walls and furniture in the front room. In the kitchen, silver-flecked granite complemented the chef-quality stainless steel appliances. A Bichon-print apron hung on a hook by the stove. Two partially-finished white wine glasses stood out on the kitchen bar.

I didn't want to know, but I asked anyway. "Don't tell me Howard...?"

Rayelle's nod as she rushed Bayle to the sink triggered Sandy's *hmm*. She drew her phone as if it were a six-shooter. "I'd better call Mrs. B."

A lawyer seemed the more prudent choice than calling my aunt, but I didn't argue. Howard's involvement affected Uncle G's objectivity.

Rayelle scrubbed Bayle's feet before speaking. "I-I didn't kill Ward. You have to believe me." Of course I believed her. She was no killer. Rayelle fed strays of all persuasions.

"How did you know Howard?" I'd always thought of Howard Looc as "Howard," though "Ward" seemed more fitting. And too familiar for a thirty-day acquaintance. Could she have known him before moving to Barkview?

"We met nine years ago at a flyball tournament," Rayelle explained. "Bayle's mom was a FGDCh. A flyball grand champion," she added, no doubt reading my blank stare. "Do you know what flyball is?"

Of course, Sandy's ponytail bobbed. I swear she knew everything.

"Guessing it's not a ball that kills flies," I said.

"It's a four-dog relay race. Each dog jumps four hurdles, catches a ball launched from a box, and races back. The trick is in the timing. The next dog can't start until the previous one crosses the finish line," Sandy explained. "Jack Russell Terriers are particularly proficient at the game."

"That box Bayle plays with?" I asked.

"Yes. Ward tweaked it for Bayle. He's fast over the hurdles but struggles with the ball release. Bolt is a grand champion. Ward asked me to join his team for the tournament next month. He said he was a strategic dog short."

"Quite a coincidence your sorority sister offers you a job at the same time," Sandy remarked. Thanks to Uncle G's training, my no-such-thing-as-a-coincidence radar activated. Did Rayelle have another agenda? We had been talking about doing a dog cooking show for years. Why had she finally agreed?

"It's not a coincidence. Ward's been talking about this"— her hands opened to encompass the room—"dogtopia for as long as I've known him. I finally decided it was time to leave the restaurant business and entirely focus on dogs." I believed her; after all, who could fake a girl-next-door blush like that?

"Morning, Mrs. B," Sandy chirped. "Sorry to bother you, but..." Sandy handed me the phone. "She wants to talk to you."

Of course my aunt did. I took the phone. "Howard Looc is dead. Send Mark to Bichon Bisquets. The murder weapon appears to be Rayelle's Bichon knife."

"I understand, dear." I figured Aunt Char did when she disconnected the call with no further comment. KDOG's corporate lawyer would have to represent Rayelle until a criminal lawyer could be retained.

I noted Rayelle's TV-friendly complexion had turned ashen. Said aloud, the evidence looked bad. "We're just being careful, Rayelle. You remember Mark from when you signed the contracts, right?" I waited for her nod. "No talking to anyone until he arrives. He will make sure everything is legal."

"But I didn't do anything."

Bayle's high-pitched bark announced Uncle G's arrival. "Then you have nothing to be worried about." His gaze swept the room, honing in on the wine glasses. Not an auspicious start.

I glared back. "Mark is on his way. No questions without him present."

Uncle G's cough did not fully disguise his cuss. He faced Rayelle. "Are you invoking your right to an attorney?"

I nodded at Rayelle's questioning look. "I guess."

"Yes or no?" With his arms crossed, Uncle G might as well be the Rock of Gibraltar.

"Y-yes."

He motioned All-American officer Richie Richardson inside. "No one touches anything in here." Uncle G's sweeping gesture included both Sandy and me. "You two, out. No witness collaboration."

When Sandy jumped to attention, the redheaded officer overwhelming the doorway startled. Six feet and a bunch more in height, Richie's linebacker build intimidated everyone on sight. Fortunately, his Boy-Scout-at-heart persona inhibited his interrogation skills.

Sandy bit her lip. She didn't want to leave Rayelle either. "What do we do?" she whispered for my ears only.

I wish I knew. As it stood, I'd be a witness for the prosecution. "Mark will be here soon."

"Please. Help me," Rayelle pleaded.

I hugged her close and whispered, "Where are the surveillance recordings?" I had to see them first.

"Ward installed the app on my phone..."

I motioned to Sandy to pick up Bayle. Aloud, I said, "Group hug."

"What is the website?" I whispered.

"I don't know. My phone is on my nightstand." Rayelle whispered her password.

Uncle G cleared his throat. "Sometime this year."

Not exactly encouraging. Never great in an emergency, I blanked. Sandy saved the day. She shoved the squirming dog into my arms. "You'd better take Bayle."

I wasn't sure who'd faint first, Rayelle or me. Bayle's yelp summed up his displeasure.

"You keep him until Rayelle knows what's going on. I'll get Bayle's brushes from the bedroom. He needs to be brushed daily."

"Daily?" My voice squeaked.

"It relaxes me," Rayelle explained.

"Rayelle, please pack his food. I know he has a special diet." Sandy overrode any possible objection with sheer will. I'd taught her well.

Uncle G's acquiescence did not bode well. An orange jumpsuit would not complement Rayelle's complexion. He motioned Sandy toward the bedroom. I nudged Rayelle. "What do I do?"

Rayelle seemed more focused. She packed numerous colored containers in a cooler with gel ice. "Bayle has a very sensitive stomach. Breakfast is in the yellow containers. Dinner in the blue. Red has snacks. Feed him one cup..."

This was even more complicated than feeding my aunt's champion Cavalier King Charles, Renny. "Geez, I need to write this down." I pulled my life-organizing, rainbow Post-it pad from my pocket and scribbled midair in Uncle G's direction. "Can I borrow a pen?"

If his compliance speed indicated the degree of trouble

Rayelle faced, Bayle would be a permanent guest. Seven Post-its later, one stuck on each container, I had assessed Rayelle's dog-insanity rating at a solid twelve. Poaching instructions for Bayle's fish? Get real.

I shifted Bayle from my right hip to my left, spitting his fluff-top out of my mouth during the transfer. This beast outweighed my aunt's Cavalier by at least five pounds. Not to mention the wet feet soaking through my top.

Uncle G's bright-eyed amusement didn't help any. "Would you mind carrying the food?" I asked him. I couldn't ask Sandy. She already carried the video camera in one hand and the two reusable bags loaded with brushes, toys and I could only guess what else in the other. Confirmation that she'd accessed Rayelle's security information likely saved me from an "obstructing the investigation" charge. I'd deal with the consequences of previewing the evidence later.

Rayelle and Bayle's tearful goodbye touched me. No wonder the dog snorted and squirmed in my incapable hands.

Uncle G lifted the cooler. "Not a word." He motioned Richie to escort us downstairs. Burdened with a struggling Bichon, I clipped Mark Wilton in the stairway as he edged past me. Horn-rimmed glasses askew, he managed to steady my tumble and murmur, "Good morning, Miss Wright." At least the delay had worked.

Between the floodlights and the crowd, it might as well have been high noon on Sycamore Street. Yellow police tape set a perimeter around Bichon Bisquets' entrance. Rayelle's competitors had certainly come out in force. I spotted Stephanie's Blue Bay Shepherd at the Third Street barricade and Mel and Nell at the Oak Street roundabout. Tina Looc's absence didn't bode well for anyone.

I looped Bayle's leash around my wrist and put him on the ground. What was the deal with carrying dogs anyway? They had four capable legs of their own. Bayle sat on my feet, literally, pressed against my leg, and whined. No translation needed. He didn't want to leave.

Sandy's fingers disappeared into his powder-puff head. "Sorry, boy." She stood, camera ready on her shoulder. "Ready to film a spot for *The Bark View*? This is serious news."

I handed Bayle's leash to Richie. "Hold him for a minute, will you?" I wove through the outdoor café tables and stood directly beneath the Bichon Bisquets sign. Sandy acknowledged my nod and set up the wide-angle lens.

Good thing Uncle G remained upstairs. Richie's indulgent smile appeared unaware as I made a project of fluffing my hair and playing with the microphone while Sandy filmed the crime scene. "I know. Shoot above the waist. Left is your best side. I mean right. My bad. Ready."

I test-counted into the mike. I knew exactly what to say. My heart beat with the familiar excitement. I loved TV. "We are here at Bichon Bisquets on Third Street to report that local entrepreneur Howard Looc has been found dead."

Uncle G exited the building as if cued. No doubt he wanted to shut me down, but I used his timely arrival to my advantage. "Chief Schmidt, please tell us what you know so far."

The silver microphone blended with his beard. "If anyone was on Third Street near Sycamore after 10 p.m. this evening, I want to talk to you."

"Thank you. Please contact Chief Schmidt or call KDOG's On the Scent tip line with any information. Remember the safety and security of our town is a community effort. This is Cat Wright on the scent." I smiled. I couldn't help myself. Reporting always felt right. I noted Uncle G had replaced Richie holding Bayle's leash. "Pack up, Sandy. We need to get to editing to make the morning show." I shooed her to her car.

Uncle G wasn't confiscating either my footage or the surveillance recordings.

I gritted my teeth, fully expecting an earful. "What? This won't air until you give me the okay. I didn't report any specifics." I didn't envy him the task of informing Tina one bit.

"Next time, ask to take photos." Uncle G handed me the leash. I really hated getting caught.

"She didn't do it," I said defensively.

"Maybe. Maybe not. I can't stop you from looking into this, but watch yourself, Cat. Howard Looc was a complicated man. Killed by someone who knew how to use a knife," Uncle G warned.

A violin-case-carrying gangster popped into my head. The sudden lump in my throat felt apple-sized. He'd put me on notice. "How do you know?"

"The coroner will need to confirm, but the knife angle and depth indicate a better-than-passing familiarity with anatomy."

Or dumb luck and I knew how he felt about coincidence. I shivered. "I'm willing to trade."

"I thought you might be. Ten a.m. at my office," he said.

"I'll bring treats for Max and Maxine. Aunt Char sent Mark," I added.

"I know. He told me."

The less said, the better, on my part. I beat a tactful retreat. Mountains of data waited at the studio.

CHAPTER 3

My head pounded from Bayle's high-pitched whine-bark when I finally parked at the KDOG studio. Despite not speaking fluent dog, I got the message loud and clear. He wanted Rayelle. How in the world did I explain this one?

Aunt Char's car in her designated space beside mine didn't bode well, either. The queen of you-need-your-beauty-sleep here at 3 a.m. added up to trouble.

I stroked Bayle's fluffy head. "You're going to have to trust me."

Or not. The dog's woeful brown eyes didn't give an inch. Censured by a neurotic cotton ball? I opened the passenger door. "Come, Bayle." His front paws hovered at the edge, shaking in what I interpreted as anticipation, but he didn't jump. He just whimpered.

A cat obeyed better. I scooped him into my arms and placed him on the ground while I unlocked the metal employee entrance door and took the elevator to the second floor. Renny, my aunt's champion Cavalier King Charles Spaniel, greeted us with a regal shake of her head and a long, not-so-flattering look at Bayle, who promptly quit whining and took refuge behind my calves.

The queen Cavalier cowed with a single stare. I scratched the breed-perfect spot atop her head, wondering if I should thank her or protect Bayle.

Aunt Char saved the day. She breezed into the hallway in St. John casual couture and coaxed Bayle to her side with what smelled suspiciously like Renny's preferred chicken treat. "Oh, Bayle. You must be so worried." Aunt Char swept him into her arms and hugged him, her white-blonde hair lost behind all that fluff.

"What are you doing here?" I didn't mean to scold. After the smoke inhalation scare during the Cavalier investigation, I tended to be overprotective.

"I thought you could use my help," Aunt Char said.

"At 3 a.m.?" Or was this about the clandestine business arrangements with Howard she'd admitted to during my last investigation?

Aunt Char carried a now-purring—no kidding—Bayle into her office without a word. I scrambled after her into what could best be described as a nineteenth-century English country house library. From the book-lined walls to the wing-back leather chairs, the room screamed tradition. Only the seasonal yellow-and-white chrysanthemum and daisy bouquet and a mystic crystal atop the desk revealed Aunt Char's style.

I heard feverish typing long before I located Sandy's towhead half-hidden behind the computer screen.

"Tell me you've wrapped up the case," I said.

"We-l-l..."

"Rayelle's competitors need a good old-fashioned spank-ing," Aunt Char remarked. Bayle squirmed off her lap. He ran a few feet, turned around, and barked once, twice. Each woof just about exploded in my already-pounding head.

"What is it, Bayle?" Aunt Char crouched to Bayle's eye level. "What?"

Renny and I shared a groan. The Cavalier sat sphinx-style on the floor and covered her head with her paws. What I wouldn't give for noise-protecting floppy ears right now.

"He wants you to throw a ball." Sandy's typing continued uninterrupted.

"It's the middle of the night," I growled.

Aunt Char pulled a spongy pink golf ball from her desk drawer and tossed it across the carpet. Bayle took off with a flapping tail. After three throws, he curled up on her lap and snored.

"He just needed to release some nervous energy," Aunt Char said. "Sleep, sweet boy. It will look better in the morning."

I doubted that. "How did you know?"

"He's a Bichon, dear. Short bursts of energy followed by cuddling. He's a little sweetheart." Aunt Char's French manicured nails peeked in and out of Bayle's poof.

"Renny is a genetic couch potato. Why do you even have a ball in your desk drawer?" I asked.

Aunt Char's half-smile portended a preparedness lecture. "What did you find out about Rayelle's competitors?" I asked Sandy quickly.

"At 11:02 p.m. last night, a floppy-hatted woman that I'd bet a Jack & Seven was Mel shook a Coke and tossed it at the front door," Sandy replied. "Pretty juvenile if you ask me, but effective if she was trying for an ant invasion."

I brushed the straw-like spot on my shoulder. So, that's what I'd gotten on my shirt when Bolt knocked me over.

"Has to be Stephanie's dog dropping a manila envelope on

the doorstep at 11:17," Sandy said. "The lighting is distorting the pixelation. Features appear Shepherdish."

"A criminal dog?" Only in Barkview.

"More like a revolving mischief door," Aunt Char stated with a huff.

"The pâté had to have been from Tina," I said, since the remaining competitors had been accounted for.

"Pâté?" Aunt Char asked.

"I stepped in it when I left Bichon Bisquets at 9:05 p.m. I thought it was dog-doo." None of the pranks explained Howard's murder, though.

Aunt Char's *hmmm* spoke volumes. "This is not acceptable in the friendliest town in America."

"The dog friendliest," I corrected her. Ask me and I'll tell you all about Barkview's fixation on those who did not fit the mold. I swear my accumulated citations financed the downtown library. Failure to yield to an oncoming Pekingese. Parking in the Paw Zone. Who knew white-spotted curbs were reserved for dog conveniences like carriages, wagons, or skateboards?

"I will speak to the mayor about that," Aunt Char said. "Jealousy is not acceptable."

"Neither is destruction of property," I added. "It's Uncle G's job to stop this."

"I will speak with him as well. Rayelle is not a murderer." Aunt Char sounded so convincing.

"Whoever did it intentionally incriminated Rayelle," Sandy remarked.

Aunt Char's next question drew my attention. "Have you asked yourself why Barkviewians haven't taken to Rayelle?"

"About a thousand times. It makes no sense. Rayelle's an over-the-top dog lover. Donates to dog-rehab charities. She's brought new business to Barkview."

"Yet she might as well own a Siamese cat," Sandy added.

I plopped into the chair beside Renny. "It's me, isn't it?"

Of course, Aunt Char's serene smile didn't waver. I really hated her revelations.

I exhaled. "I hired an outsider for a show when I had potential talent in Barkview to draw from."

"But not one of the Barkview biscuiteers are TV material," Sandy insisted. "Mel crashed and burned in front of the camera at her *Throw Him a Bone* interview."

More like freaked out on my aunt's cable show. The second the green camera light had turned on, she'd darted out the emergency exit to throw up. No returning to be interviewed after that.

"Stage fright is distressing," Aunt Char pointed out.

"No film crew will work with Tina Looc if there's a knife within throwing distance. And Stephanie's surfer-dude vocabulary isn't exactly mainstream," Sandy said, completing her summary of possible replacements for Rayelle.

Or particularly understandable without Google translation. I liked Stephanie McCarthy, but her Frosted Pup's Creamery catered to the cowabunga surfing crowd. "I should've at least interviewed for the position before hiring my sorority sister." I had with Sandy. No one had wanted to be my assistant after I'd run a few folks through the paces. She'd been accepted with awe, likely for tolerating me. My own arrogance and programming excitement had contributed to this rift.

"You have an opportunity to correct the situation. Embrace it, my dear. You don't often get a second chance," Aunt Char announced.

I dropped my elbows to the desk and held my hammering head steady. My star chef was being questioned in a murder investigation. If that wasn't bad enough, I only had one episode taped. Begging the question: who was going to cook for *Fido's Food Fest* next Sunday?

Panic edged my composure. I had to get Rayelle out of trouble fast.

Aunt Char read my mind. "Sandy and I will take over your producing duties until Rayelle is cleared. In fact, this might be a good time for me to tape additional segments."

"You don't have time to babysit the studio." I had to object. With the mayoral election only a month away, Aunt Char politicked every spare minute for the job.

"Family first," Aunt Char said. "The rest will work itself out."

Or not. "Tell me there was something helpful on the recordings." I needed something...anything to latch onto.

"Howard Looc adjusted the camera angle at 11:32, kicked a Coke can aside, picked up an envelope, and then went inside," Sandy explained.

That made no sense. Why would he pick up the envelope and not the Coke can?

"Look." Sandy turned the screen toward us. Both Aunt Char and I crowded in. Sure enough, Howard had rotated the camera angle away from the front door. Fortunately, he'd overlooked his reflection in the glass.

"The really interesting part is that at 11:47, an ethereal, iridescent blob opens the door and floats in. It leaves at 11:59."

Before I could accuse her of B-movie antics, Sandy fast-forwarded the recording. Aunt Char's hand rested on my shoulder as she, too, looked on.

"Focus on the shadow near the door." Sandy pointed to what could easily pass as an aberration in the window. "It looks like a gremlin or something."

"Creepy," I muttered. No identifying features. Not even a discernible silhouette to go on.

"You can hear Bolt barking at 11:57. That blob had to have been the murderer," Sandy said. "If I rewind to 11:16, there is faint audio of Rayelle saying goodbye to Howard that you're not going to like."

As usual, Sandy nailed that one. Rayelle's insistent voice saying, "Come on, Sweetheart," followed by Howard's harsh response to "get over it," indicated far more was going on than Rayelle had admitted to.

Aunt Char and Sandy's shared look squelched any emphatic denial. Deep down I knew Rayelle couldn't murder anyone. Unfortunately, that conversation snippet, the murder weapon, the countertop wine glasses—never mind that brainiac Howard fit Rayelle's preferred dating profile—pointed right at her.

"I know Rayelle. There is no way she did this." I aimed to convince. I needed them to believe, too.

Aunt Char's warm hand rested on mine. "I believe you, my dear. Besides, that blob can't possibly be Rayelle. She's much taller."

Sandy's hand topped Aunt Char's in solidarity. "I agree."

Their support meant everything. I exhaled, not realizing I'd been holding my breath.

"You're right about the blob seeming smaller, but Rayelle practically lives in stilettos. She could also be slouching to appear shorter," Sandy said. "Theoretically, she'd just quarreled with Howard. She knew the cameras were recording. She knew he was in her shop."

No doubt Uncle G's thought process as well. "What could cause that blob?"

"Maybe a reflective jacket. They do kinda look translucent in low light." Sandy read my confusion. "You know, like the crinkly reflective material in cycling or running attire. I wear a jacket like that when I walk Jack in the dark."

"Really?"

"A safety must," Aunt Char added.

I flopped into a wing-back chair. "Forget the blob for a second. The whole scenario makes no sense. Why would Howard have an argument with Rayelle and then go into her shop and sit in the dark for twenty minutes?"

No answer to that.

"He entered after he picked up the envelope. He could've been waiting for someone," Sandy suggested.

"Why meet at Bichon Bisquets? Howard lives at a no-questions-asked casino," I said.

"Did Rayelle enter or leave?" Aunt Char asked.

"The recording doesn't show the apartment's doorway. Only a reflection of the blob entering and leaving the shop," Sandy said.

"The apartment has a front and back entrance," Aunt Char said. "Is there…"

"The back camera was either disabled or not set up. I can't tell. For all we know, Rayelle had a fight with Howard, snuck downstairs, killed him and went to bed," Sandy replied.

Except she'd been sound asleep when the chief called her. No one is that good an actress. "Doesn't explain why Howard changed the camera angle or why he picked up the envelope Stephanie's dog dropped off or went inside the shop."

"Howard and Stephanie are an unlikely pair," Sandy remarked.

I agreed. Had Uncle G found the envelope? If he didn't know its possible importance, it could still be in the barkery.

"The circumstantial evidence against Rayelle is significant," Aunt Char said. "You need another suspect."

No kidding. Fortunately, I had a few ideas.

CHAPTER 4

How I ended up babysitting Bayle had to be a testament to effective tag teaming or really limited choices.

"Just talk to him." Aunt Char's answer to everything dog-related seriously lacked practicality.

"And tell him what? That his mom is in trouble?" I'd earned my peevishness after nineteen hours on the go.

"Heavens, no. Tell him you need his help."

Another promising suggestion. Naturally, Sandy agreed with Aunt Char. As if Sandy's dog-whispering skills could be relied upon. Her Jack Russell ran circles around her.

"What are you afraid of?" Trust Aunt Char to get to the heart of the issue.

"I-I am not..."

My aunt crossed her arms. "A dog person. Please, Cat. You are a responsible adult. Renny thrived under our care."

By whose definition? Renny buried her head beneath her paws, refusing to meet my eye. She remembered her ER visit after the Pit Bull attack all too well. Not a confidence booster for sure. Taking issue with "responsible" and "adult" seemed pointless since Aunt Char's dog-with-a-bone look rarely wavered.

"What if I do something wrong? I nearly killed Renny." There it was, my insecurity verbalized. Kids did the same thing to me.

Sandy's gape I expected, but not Aunt Char's telling half-smile. "You called 911 and stayed by her. Never forget that. Bayle will be fine under your care."

Not exactly the way I remembered it, but my aunt's assurance helped a little. I glared at the fluff-ball, too tired to object further. For better or worse, Bayle was with me.

We arrived at my beachfront townhouse as my Gustav Becker wall clock chimed 4 a.m. I hadn't been holding my breath that I'd hear from Rayelle by now, but I had hoped. Bayle must've been as exhausted as I was because his cursory sniff barely acknowledged my jungle-cat décor as he followed me into my bedroom. He jumped into my bed and snuggled up to a pillow before my shoes hit the floor.

I'm not even sure if he snored. A blast of light woke me from a dead sleep what felt like five minutes later. Truthfully, it was closer to seven and Bayle, the alarm dog, had nosed open the exact right blind. He needed to go out. At least that's what I figured his leaping like a jumping bean meant.

Five minutes later, my toes wiggled on the damp cement boardwalk while I fantasized about my first cup of coffee. Luckily, I'd thrown on my new jaguar-print pj's, the ones with lace trim that doubled as a yoga outfit, since every passing eye noticed us. News of Bayle's new lodgings would spread faster than an October wildfire.

I smoothed my hair and tested my morning breath. If my distance vision could be trusted in the peekaboo morning light, J. Tracker's president, Sean Riley, led the Jack Russell running group headed my way. At least the approaching orange-red halo looked like Sean's carrot-red hair.

Between his not-so-amiably-dissolved partnership with Howard and the possible industrial espionage I'd uncovered while tracking the Cavaliers, Sean had ample motive to seek revenge. Too bad Sean and I weren't exactly besties. I had to practically trip him to get his attention.

"I see you have another temporary dog." Sean's deep voice didn't sound a bit winded despite just passing the five-mile mark. JRu, his hyperactive Jack Russell, planted his paws in front of Bayle and barked a crescendo.

I scooped up the quivering cotton ball. "I protect my friends."

"An admirable quality. But having a dog as your friend, Cat?"

"Who'd have thought? Right?" I matched his teasing smile. "We all have depths we don't show the world."

"True."

"Like your outfit. Where did you get it?" Sandy might be onto something. Under the lighting at Bichon Bisquets, Sean's silver reflective garb could've caused that eerie blob. I'd have to test it.

"It's the latest safety wear." His forefinger drew my attention to the shimmering fabric. "The material glows in fog and in the dark."

"Do you normally run at night?" Sean lived up the hill in the high-rent Barkview Terraces. Beautiful as the Pacific view was, the twisty-turny access road required diligence under ideal conditions, and especially in the evening.

"At this time of the year, there aren't always enough hours in the day." He jogged in place. "You didn't stop me to talk about my exercise routine."

"No, I..."

"If you want to know where I was last night, I was at home in bed asleep. My alarm was set. My official comment on Howard's death is that my heart goes out to Tina and his children. Off the record, Howard was a complicated man. Look into that before you throw around accusations." Sean tipped a nonexistent baseball cap and disappeared into the dozen or so Jack Russells yipping with on-the-hunt excitement.

I carried Bayle inside. Of course Howard had bones buried somewhere. Everyone did. I just had to figure out where to start digging.

Inside my small two-butt-size granite and stainless steel kitchen, I dished Bayle's labeled food into his bowl. His chicken and vegetables in gravy looked better than my chocolate protein shake. If he didn't eat it all, I'd... Never mind, he practically inhaled every bite and licked the bowl clean just to be sure.

Moments later, he dropped a yellow tennis ball at my feet and barked. A happy, playful bark? I'd lost it this time. A bark was a bark. Or was it? Bayle's air-dusting tail confirmed my hypothesis.

How could I not smile? Pure, childlike joy radiated from him as I threw the ball down the hall. Four throws later he plopped at my feet and rolled over for a belly scratch. I picked a leaf off his leg. Did his puffy fur seem flatter?

With a yawn, I poured a double caramel cappuccino into a mega-mug. The first satisfying swallow helped clear the fog. Time to review what could be critical information in exonerating Rayelle—and illicit information at that.

Fortified, I stepped over Bayle and headed to my office. Not to be left behind, he scurried after me, his nails tip-tapping on the tile.

Inspired by Ernest Hemingway's travels, an antique campaign chair, a leather-pad inlaid table that doubled as a desk, a file drawer, and two overflowing bookshelves filled the room. I removed an old-school digital camera from the bottom file drawer and plugged it into the USB port on my computer. With Howard dead, no one could question exactly how I'd obtained this information. Breaking-and-entering Howard's room at the Indian casino while tracking the Cavaliers had been pure insanity. Who'd have guessed that the data that had appeared to be questionable intel on Petronics and J. Tracker might matter now?

Analyzing the information on a computer screen didn't help much. The two mechanical drawings looked like haphazard lines on graph paper. Laid atop each other, the drawings appeared to be identical. Could this be the secret subcutaneous chip? The chip that not only tracked dogs, but also monitored their health that Aunt Char had funded with Howard?

No way my straight-shooter aunt could be tied to another murder. A panic attack threatened as I scanned the documents. Except for the competing logos, the documents appeared identical, right down to the same inventor's name in the lower right-hand corner. Who was F. Hazing, exactly? Neither J. Tracker nor Petronics employed him.

Could an independent contractor have sold the drawings to both companies? A quick Google search of F. Hazing found nothing. Facebook netted a few hits. No matches with the initial F. No businesses or obvious inventors. This was a job for Sandy's extraordinary computer skills.

No doubt Uncle G knew something. The wall clock bonged nine times, reminding me of our impending meeting. I quickly dressed in black trousers and a KDOG oxford shirt and was dashing on lipstick when Russ called. The man's I-need-to-talk-to-you radar was uncanny. "You're not going to believe what's going on," I warned him.

"Good morning to you, too." His deep chuckle warmed me. Since he lived and worked in Los Angeles, our together time tended to be on weekends. The ninety-mile separation always seemed farther on Monday morning.

"Sorry."

Bayle barked before I could explain.

"Is that...?"

"Bayle. You remember... Never mind. You remember everything." He did, too.

"I'm afraid to ask how it's going."

In his shoes I'd say the same thing. The last dog I'd cared for had been Renny—incognito—and what a mess that had been. "I have the little beast until... Hang on." Bayle dropped the ball at my feet. I tossed it down the hall, my eye oddly drawn to his bouncing fluff. "Howard Looc has been murdered."

"I know. The chief called me."

"What? Why?" Russ specialized in child abduction cases with the FBI.

"What happened to 'I'm excited to speak to you, Russ?'"

What indeed? "I am, of course, but why are you involved?"

"The chief has asked me to investigate Howard Looc's murder."

Why would Barkview hire an expensive consultant-detective instead of borrowing a detective from the somewhat nearby San Diego Police Department? My gut screamed there was more to it, the same gut Russ had taught me to trust. "And you're just dropping everything...?"

"Not exactly. You know my team is tying up a case in San Diego."

That had been his excuse to come south for months now. I hadn't doubted him. He'd never given me a reason to...yet. I couldn't put my finger on why I wasn't convinced now.

"Sounds like you've accepted," I said. No denial. The silence stretched between us, not by design on my part. Truthfully, too many possible outcomes flashed through my mind.

"I'd hoped you'd be happy to see more of me."

Sexy and exciting Russ underfoot? My pulse should be doing backflips. Yet caution flared. The same caution I'd felt the last time Howard Looc's name came up. "What's going on here, Russ?"

It didn't take a clairvoyant to sense his disappointment. "Since my answer is obviously going to define our relationship moving forward, we'll talk when I get there."

I felt like a heel for not disagreeing. Was I overreacting? Russ worked in a need-to-know world. He should expect my loyalty, but secrets demanded answers.

CHAPTER 5

I pulled into the Daily Wag Coffee Bar about half an hour later. The corner Victorian, built in 1907 in the classic, whitewashed gingerbread style, was decked out in a Halloween Casper-the-Friendly-Ghost theme. From ghosts floating on the lattice to baby blush roses in spectral bud vases on wrought-iron tables, the decorations on the spindle porch fronting the Second and Maple Street roundabout obeyed every Barkview Halloween ordinance.

In a dog-dominated town, a holiday designed to frighten had to be legislated. By city council order, ringing doorbells and shouting "Trick or treat!"—and every other noise-generating, motion-activated, and loosely floating decoration—had been banned to avoid upsetting our canine inhabitants. Forget skeletons, too. Why anyone would decorate with a dog magnet in this town seemed insane.

In usual community fashion, Barkview embraced a more welcoming cartoon or autumn leaf and pumpkin theme.

Naturally, Bayle didn't appreciate the effort. He planted both paws and refused to step inside. A pull on his leash had no effect. The aroma of my steaming caramel cappuccino teased me from the marble counter. In one smooth move, I scooped him under my arm running-back style and hauled him past the murmuring gossips.

"Good morning, Cat. Bayle." Gabby Tuner handed me the tall paper cup dusted with dark chocolate.

I nodded my thanks and took a long, satisfying swallow.

Gabby's smile widened. "I swear you purr when you drink that."

No doubt. "Don't tell anyone." The wrong thing to say to the director of gossip central.

A multi-generation Barkviewian, Gabby had gone east for college, finding her calling during sophomore year all-nighters. Ten years later, she shaped public opinion one bombshell at a time.

"So, what's the street's opinion on Howard's murder?" I might as well get right to it.

Gabby readjusted the ghost-braided headband containing her flowing chestnut hair. "Mostly stunned. I mean, Howard was an"—her pause drew me in—"interesting man. They feel for Tina and the kids." She stroked the Saluki, Sal, hugging her left side. A true owner-dog look-alike pair, their lanky, angular features brought a strung-out caffeine junkie to mind.

"Anything I should know about?"

Gabby could always be counted on for outrageous fodder. The telltale twinkle in her dark-roast-brown eyes promised a zinger. "W-e-l-l." Elbows on the counter, she leaned whisper-close. Pin-dropping silence ensued as the room listened in. "Rayelle didn't kill Howard. The Vespa Guardian did."

I joined the collective gasp. Couldn't help myself. Like information on the internet, if Gabby said it, it had to be true.

My eyes rolled to the spirit-laden ceiling. Much as I wanted Rayelle exonerated... "Really? A ghost?"

"I'm dead-dog serious." Gabby's unwavering gaze held mine. "The Vespa Guardian comes out during the crescent and new moons to protect women."

As if Barkview wasn't crazy enough. "Why haven't I heard about this guardian?" How could I have missed a Barkview ghost story?

"You didn't grow up here. Every teenager knows about the Vespa Guardian. It finds girls who stay out past curfew and, well... I can't say more."

Gotta appreciate Barkview's PTA coming up with this one. "My dad would've appreciated this ghost in my day."

"It's true. The ghost comes out at midnight to protect wayward women," Gabby said with true Hitchcockian flair.

"Don't tell me you incurred the guardian's wrath." Teenage Gabby had to have been a handful. Her actual fear tempered my amusement. More gently, I asked, "What did you see?"

"A black scooter with beady eyes and a filmy, translucent blob." She gestured toward a ceiling-bound ghost.

"How did you know it was the Vespa Guardian?"

"I'd heard stories, but when I heard the *rat-ta-ta, rat-ta-ta, vroom, rat-ta-ta*, I knew." Gabby typed something on her phone. "I'll never forget. I still have nightmares. Ah, here it is." She flashed a picture of a vintage Vespa and played the YouTube audio.

Sure enough, the sound matched her description. The story still didn't make sense. "So, why would a ghost who protects women murder Howard?"

"Maybe it was protecting Tina."

"From what?"

"He was a cheating husband."

"You realize how crazy this sounds, right?"

That truth slowed Gabby down. "I guess so, but why would

Rayelle kill Howard, anyway? I mean, she's paying nothing for her place."

I choked on my coffee.

"You know Howard owned the building. Right?"

I knew that. "Are you insinuating Rayelle wasn't paying rent?"

"Know it for a fact. She doesn't pay for a year." Envy laced that comment. "Wish I knew what she did to get that deal."

So did I. That tidbit indicated an even deeper relationship between Howard and Rayelle than I'd thought.

If Gabby knew about Howard's favorable deal with her competitor, then so did Tina. Could this really be a love triangle? "Where did you...?"

"Tsk. Tsk. You know I can't divulge my sources," Gabby warned.

I, of all people, understood protecting informants.

Gabby continued. "I can tell you that Michelle Le Fleur reported Bolt's barking. Said he was pacing like a caged tiger in the car."

Michelle lived above the Fluff and Buff Salon on Third Street, not quite a block from Howard's parked car. No doubt Bolt's barking woke her. How had she seen the dog inside the car in the dark?

"Michelle and Fifi left here a little after eight-thirty last night," Gabby offered.

Michelle's route home would have taken her right by Rayelle's shop around the time the pâté mischief occurred. "Did she see anything?"

Gabby shrugged. "You know Michelle."

The groomer-whisperer did have "drama queen" covered.

"Tina's a mess. There's no going back now," Gabby added.

"Are you saying Tina wanted to reconcile with Howard?" I asked. Had to love Gabby's information.

Gabby nodded. "She never wanted the separation to begin with. They were two peas."

"Emotional Tina and reserved Howard?" Talk about opposites.

"Maybe on the surface they weren't, but here"—Gabby tapped her heart—"where it matters, they were soul mates. Tina's words. I swear. The whole divorce shocked her."

"Divorce? Last I heard they were separated."

"Just last week Howard and Mark sat at that table"—she pointed to a guaranteed-to-be-overheard table near the entry —"and discussed the, uh, next steps."

Ultra-discreet Mark holding a private client meeting in Gabby's tell-all establishment? The whole meeting made no sense. Mark was a corporate lawyer. He didn't handle divorces either. "Did Tina know?" Dumb question. Of course she knew minutes after the meeting. Gabby couldn't keep a bomb like that quiet. Why would Howard make such a public announcement?

"She had a right to know." Gabby encroached on my personal space to whisper, "She got really quiet. Kinda scared me. You know her temper."

Point conceded. "What happened next?"

"She thanked me for calling and hung up."

"No plates breaking?"

"Not a single one." Gabby's disappointment resonated.

Passionate Tina reserved? Had she already known? Could that be a motive?

"Stephan's been a nuisance, too. Hard to believe he thinks he has a chance with Tina," Gabby added.

"Stephanie's duded-out surfer brother?" The co-owner of the Frosty Pups Creamery and adjacent Graveyards and Ghosts Tours, interested in Tina? Now, that was intriguing.

"They were Barkview High's prom king and queen."

"In 2010."

"It's been a while, but they were high school sweethearts. Their whole breakup was nasty."

"How so?" I sipped my coffee. Gabby was on a roll.

"Tina met Howard at her parents' restaurant. She claimed it was love over muttballs and extra sauce. Tina's parents flipped out. I mean, they'd forbidden her to see Stephan. You can imagine what they said about their Italian princess in love with a Chinese immigrant."

"Why did they object to Stephan?" I asked.

"Stephan didn't exactly fit the Principato mold," Gabby remarked.

I didn't ask why. There had to be more to this. Tina had married Howard despite her parents' objections.

"Tina's mom swears the whole Howard thing put Tina's dad in an early grave."

"More likely the artery-clogging fried calamari and tiramisu were to blame," I couldn't help commenting.

Gabby didn't miss a beat. "Stephan swore Howard coerced Tina into marrying him."

Tina being coerced into anything seemed out of character. "This is the twenty-first century."

"Not in an old-school Catholic family."

"She's free now," I remarked.

"She is. Back in high school, Stephan was this hot surfer. Not so much now."

Barkview's entrepreneur of the year Tina with *broski* Stephan? That one just didn't track. Unrequited love could equal motive, though. I mentally added Stephan to my talk-to list.

"I'm heading to police headquarters... Can I have a double espresso for Uncle G?" No doubt he'd need it.

Gabby handed me the espresso and packed two doggie

treats for Max and Maxine in a printed paper sack with handles. "What about Bayle?" I hoped I sounded conversational. Every dog got a Daily Biscuit. Was this doggie discrimination?

"Oh, no! Rayelle would have my head. That dog has pancreatitis."

I glanced at the picture of perfect health sticking his pink tongue at me. "He looks fine."

"Now he does. When his pancreas gets inflamed it causes all kinds of nasty problems." Gabby's nose scrunched.

I blanched. "Nasty like what?"

"Trust me." She patted my wrist. "It's not something you want to deal with."

Cleaning up after a sick dog? Ugh! I hadn't signed up for that.

"That's why Rayelle feeds him a special diet. Didn't you know Bayle inspired her to become a chef?" Gabby asked.

Rayelle had told me that. That Gabby knew said a lot about ultra-private Rayelle's relationship with the woman.

"You need to be careful what he eats. Any little thing could trigger the condition," Gabby warned me. "And kill him."

No pressure here. I swallowed. Just great. Only a day and a half of Bayle's special food remained in my refrigerator. I cooked Asian fusion. Probably not on Bayle's approved food list. Rayelle needed to be back in her kitchen fast.

CHAPTER 6

I arrived at police headquarters precisely at ten. Four empty coffee cups littered Uncle G's desktop, explaining his pacing, bloodshot eyes, and the pinwheeling toothpick in his mouth, but not the red welt above his left eye.

I gave Max and Maxine their treats and reluctantly handed Uncle G another coffee cup. Bayle snuggled on my lap in the leather side chair. "Why are you still holding Rayelle?"

"Other than evidence?" His growl confirmed his bearish demeanor.

"I have it on good authority that the Vespa Guardian has struck."

Uncle G's glare flayed me in a single swoop. So much for the ghost defense. Post-its ready, I swiped a pen from his fancy personalized penholder the moment he turned away. "Your evidence is circumstantial."

"I have a taped argument. Wine glasses in the accused's apartment. Murder weapon with her fingerprints on it. Sugar-daddy apartment. Open-and-shut lovers quarrel," Uncle G said.

If it was only that simple. "So, if they were upstairs drinking wine, how did she get the body downstairs and into that position in the chair? Howard outweighed Rayelle by ninety-plus pounds. Why did he leave his dog in his car? What about the money? You always tell me to follow the money." After all, that investigative method worked on TV. "What does Rayelle gain from Howard's death?"

Uncle G sat in his cavernous swivel chair, oddly still. "Not a thing. Tina Looc and his children are Howard's primary beneficiaries."

"Tina did go after Howard with a knife," I pointed out.

"It was a paring knife."

Not exactly with killer intent... that time. "She's still volatile. And financially has the most to gain. She knew Howard intended to file for divorce."

"Her alibi checks out. Security footage shows Tina and her mother working at Ciao Bella until after midnight. It was Muttballs night."

As if bring-your-dog-to-dinner night explained it all.

"Her grandmother watched the kids until Tina carried them to her car at 12:09 a.m."

"The kids were up late."

"They sleep at grandma's apartment above the restaurant until Tina takes them home after she closes for the night."

Hard to believe the kids slept through the move. "Is the restaurant closed?" I asked.

"No. Tina wanted to keep busy."

That sounded very much like Tina. "How did she react to Howard's death?"

"Tears. General hysteria. Richie's sworn off women." Uncle G's grimace indicated there was more to it.

I pointed to the welt on his forehead. "Plate?" Airborne plates tended to solve life's challenges at Ciao Bella Italiano.

"A flyball trophy."

My snicker just blurted out despite Uncle G's wounded-bear growl. "Rayelle said Howard lobbied for Bayle to join his flyball team."

"Howard's team is the reigning state champion. They finished second at Nationals last year. Bayle is Howard's short dog."

My ignorance must've shown. Uncle G explained further. "The hurdles' height is set to the shortest dog's ability to jump. That box behind Rayelle's counter is a spring-loaded flyball launcher."

"Rayelle said Howard modified it for Bayle. Apparently, Bayle's mom was a Grand something." Uncle G's nod confirmed Gabby's words. "How do you know so much about this? I've never heard of flyball until last night." Or was it this morning?

"You should get out more. Barkview has three nationally ranked competing teams."

Most towns had a bowling league. "Really? Who else is involved?"

"Nell and Mel's Fur in a Blur is ranked in the top ten this year. Sean Riley's Tracker's Packers is fifteenth."

Interesting connection. "That must be some rivalry."

"You have no idea. Tina's dog runs with Sean's team now."

"And you have *Rayelle* in custody?" Sean teaming up with Howard's just-about-ex-wife spelled bad with a capital B.

"See for yourself. Practice is at Barklay Park Tuesday night."

Not a prayer. My ears hurt just walking a block from that hound playground. "Sean tells me he was home alone asleep last night during the murder."

"He was. His security company reported his alarm was set

at 9:06 p.m. and turned off at 6:22 a.m. No activity recorded on the exterior motion-detector cameras all night."

"That's hardly an alibi," I said.

Uncle G's brow-lifting scowl delivered his opinion.

I returned the look. Bayle took offense. He leaped to his full twenty-four-inch height and growled in true Napoleonic fervor.

Max wasn't taking any of it. His deep, room-vibrating bark escalated the tension. I grabbed Bayle. A marshmallow in the world of German Shepherd snacks, intervention seemed prudent. "Enough. Bayle, no."

Uncle G motioned Max to sit with a flick of his wrist. Crisis averted and an opening for me, if Uncle G's yawn counted in my favor.

"Why did you call Russ?" I asked.

"I need an investigator."

"A child abduction specialist?"

"Are you questioning my call?" Uncle G asked.

Interesting misdirect. Was there more to this than a murder? Uncle G knew more than he was saying. "Just your motive."

"Doc's got George out another six weeks."

Barkview's resident detective's surgery recovery seemed lengthy. "All the more reason to call San Diego PD for help."

"Russ is the right man for the job," the chief insisted.

"You're interfering."

"Your personal life is not the issue here." He'd said too much. A testament to his exhaustion.

On offense, I leaned forward. "What is the issue, then?"

Another glare. "That is need-to-know."

I pointed to my tightly latched briefcase. "If you want my help, I need to know."

He settled into his chair. I braced for his good-old-boy lecture, unbending.

"Now, Cat..."

"Don't you dare 'Now, Cat' me. You have my star chef in jail."

"She is just being questioned."

"So she can leave at any time."

Uncle G's shrug suggested otherwise. The arraignment clock didn't start until she'd been officially detained. Bayle's head cocked to the side. No way he'd understood. "You're ruining her business and reputation."

"I'm protecting her."

"From whom?"

No answer. Uncle G wasn't offering a thing. I still had leverage. If I played my cards right, I could ask questions until he shut me down. "Aunt Char invested in the new Petronics' dog tracker. Is she in danger?"

His double take made my stomach flutter. "The mayoral election is a month away. Is there nothing she isn't involved in?"

"You know Aunt Char. The investment was made on behalf of the Barkview Humane Society." Not exactly a straight answer. "Well? Is she in danger?"

"No. I'll talk to her, though."

"Did Howard have any gambling debts?" I asked.

"No. Howard had an eidetic memory. Cards were a game to him."

"He counted cards?" The casino had to love that.

"He memorized the cards and played the odds. He won more often than he lost. The casino wins on the play he attracts."

Nothing from that angle. Maybe the patent information I'd

discovered in Howard's hotel room mattered. "How many patents did he have?"

Uncle G scratched his chin. "I don't know exactly."

I struck dog heaven with that one. "Did J. Tracker steal Howard's collar patent?"

"The lawsuit was settled out of court. The terms are not in the public record. Howard did receive a large payoff from J. Tracker."

Sean would know why. "Who is F. Hazing?"

Did Uncle G flinch, or had I imagined it? It happened so fast. "Where did you hear that?" His toothpick seemed to pause, waiting for my answer.

F. Hazing was important. "It's in the documents I, uh, found."

Uncle G unfolded his long legs and stood. Interrogation over. "I'm going to the men's room. When I get back, anything on my desk will be viewed as having come from an anonymous source."

I left the data on his blotter and walked through the officers' cubicles to the visitor's entrance to see Rayelle. Considering my involvement, I half expected to be denied visitation. The simple sign-in process for both Bayle and me took me by surprise. Only in Barkview could a dog be considered family.

Five minutes later I sat across a particleboard table in a white interview room as sterile as a hospital, with the kind of two-way mirror I'd seen on TV. My Post-its and the pen I'd swiped from Uncle G ready, I waited. Suddenly, Bayle barked and scrambled to the door, pacing. Rayelle made it only partway inside when the dog leaped into her open arms. His defection chafed, oddly. I should have been relieved.

They belonged together. Bayle licking Rayelle's face reminded me of Renny and my aunt. I didn't need to understand, just accept. Why did a weird bereavement persist?

Afraid we were on borrowed time, I shook it off and got right to business. "We have a problem."

"Just one?" Rayelle's wry humor drew my smile.

"Your video surveillance tapes show Howard leaving your apartment. You are saying, 'Come on, Sweetheart.' Howard responds, 'Get over it.'"

Rayelle bit her lip. Her eyes darted up and to the left. A good sign. "I wasn't talking to Ward. I was calling Bayle. He wasn't obeying me."

No surprise there. My neck muscles relaxed. The dialogue made sense in that context.

"Ward disagreed with disciplining Bayle. He felt punishing him would stifle his exuberance."

Mr. Order and Procedure Looc against behavior modification? I glared at the cuddle-bug in Rayelle's arms. She crossed her heart. "I swear. Couldn't believe it either."

I made a note of that inconsistency. "How well do you know Michelle Le Fleur?"

"Best groomer I've ever used. She seems a little high strung. Why?"

"She reported Bolt barking. She said she saw him in Howard's car."

"That's strange. She walked by around 9:30. We traded waves while I was trying to sync the security cameras. The lights went out in her apartment well before ten. Ward hadn't even arrived yet. I don't know how she could've seen the car from her apartment anyway."

Something to check. "She said she's seen Howard's car parked there often."

"I told you he stops by once in a while."

"She indicated it's more like once or twice a week."

It didn't take a degree in psychology to read Rayelle's surprise. "Is everyone in Barkview in everyone else's business?"

"Uh, yes. This isn't LA." A defensive redirect? What was she hiding? Was there more to Rayelle and Howard after all?

"No, it is not." Her rueful headshake could mean anything. "There's something off about Michelle. She says she's Parisian, but her accent is Flemish."

Another redirect or clue? "Really? How can you tell?" I made a note. Her charmingly accented English sounded French to me, but it made sense there were different dialects.

"I spent a year at Le Cordon Bleu in Paris. My roommate was from Brugge, Belgium." Did her hand quiver as she stroked Bayle?

Even I knew that was one of the best cooking schools in the world. "You never told me."

"I know. It was right after the dog attacked you. You were in a bad place. By the time you were better, I'd moved on. I wanted to cook for dogs. The snobs didn't get it." Rayelle's contented smile said she had no regrets.

I squeezed her hand. Snotty Michelin-Guide land must've thought she'd lost it.

"I suppose she could've heard Bolt barking," Rayelle said. "I don't know why Ward parked there. He always did when he visited. He usually came by after flyball practice on Tuesdays, mostly to brag about the team and show me the practice video. He never stayed for more than forty minutes. Last night was odd. I swear he checked his watch ten times while we visited."

"Like he had a meeting?" I'd felt the same with Rayelle.

"Maybe."

"Why didn't you tell me Howard was coming over?"

"In retrospect, it was stupid. I just didn't want to explain our relationship."

I wanted to believe her, but her flush said there was more. "Did he have a key?"

"Of course." Her voice caught. "Let me clarify. He is—was

my landlord. I did not give him the key to visit me." She wiped a tear. "The great deal he offered me on the property helped get me established here. I suppose it looks like he bought me. It was about Bayle. Not me. Ward lost a bet to the number one Sacramento flyball team. He didn't lose well."

No kidding. "What about Sean Riley?"

Rayelle inhaled. "Hard to believe those two are grown men. I don't know the details of the lawsuit, and frankly I don't want to know. After the settlement, Sean became obsessed with beating Ward's flyball team. I still can't believe he recruited Tina's dog."

"How did Howard take it?"

"You'd think badly, but he just laughed. He said if Sean want his leftovers, he was welcome to them."

"I don't understand. Are Sean and Tina involved?"

"I don't know. All I can say is Tina and Sean deserve each other."

Talk about a telling statement. Just not exactly sure what it told yet, especially if Rayelle wasn't romantically involved with Howard. "What did Howard do?"

"He came up for a drink and then left. I had no idea he went into the shop."

Could be a meeting of sorts. "Tell me about F. Hazing."

"Who?" Her blank expression couldn't be feigned.

It was my turn to be evasive. "It was on some paperwork I found at Petronics."

"Maybe a flyball dog or team's name? The names can be wild."

Given Howard's competitive fascination, that made as much sense as anything else. I noted the idea and scrunched the Post-it in my pocket. "Any other ideas? You knew Howard better than I did."

She scratched her chin. "Well, Ward loved anagrams. You know he had a photographic memory, right?"

I nodded. That was close enough to eidetic memory for me to let it go.

"He said word games kept his mind razor-sharp."

A commotion outside the door signaled our time was up. I tried to wrap it up, but Rayelle placed her hand on mine. "The chief says I'm safer here. I don't understand what's going on. Tina is uh ... passionate, but do you think she'd really come after me?"

I shrugged. I'd never even thought of that possibility. When I recalled the ten years I'd known Tina Looc, many images came to mind. Suave businesswoman who talked with her hands, plate thrower, animated, passionate, Italian. Murderer? Not exactly. She was more inclined to give you the shirt off her back.

"First, thank you for taking care of Bayle. I know he can be a handful." Her fingers snagged in his puffy hair.

"I know. I need to brush him tonight," I said quickly. We'd been lucky to make it out of the house this a.m.

Rayelle smiled. "Brushing him twice a day barely keeps up. His hair is like a Swiffer duster."

I seemed to pull a leaf off him hourly.

"Bayle has a double coat of hair. Soft guard hairs are on the outside and coarser hairs are closer to his body. It tangles worse than your hair. I swear I find treasures in his tail all the time."

"What kind of treasures?" Did I really want to know?

"Leaves and small shells I get, but chicken bones and jacks? I have no idea where he picks them up."

Great. Just what I needed: foreign objects in my house and car.

"You need to consider that this is about Bayle." Rayelle's

dead-dog seriousness stunned me silent. "You have to admit that someone has done a good job framing me. Ward basically paid me off to bring Bayle to Barkview and join his flyball team. Before Bayle even runs, Ward ends up dead in my shop after what looks like a clandestine meeting. He's killed with my knife that has only my fingerprints on it," explained Rayelle. "And yes. Bayle really is that fast."

"That's insane." Kill someone over a dog's flyball team? "What will you do now? Still run for Howard's team?"

"Maybe. I don't know. The thing is, if I'm arrested, you get Bayle."

"Me!" Thankfully I'd remained seated. My legs would've crumpled beneath me with that announcement.

"Of course. Who else would I trust my baby to?"

"How about someone who likes dogs?" In all fairness, I thought she'd been kidding. The starkness in her sky-blue gaze said otherwise.

"You like dogs. You just haven't committed to your breed yet. Bayle will win you over. I know he will."

He'd make me crazy first. Ugh. I glared at his too-innocent brown eyes. "Th-there has to be someone else."

"No. There isn't. Hey. Consider it a bigger incentive to get me out of here." Despite her bravado, Rayelle's hand shook as she stroked Bayle. "I have another problem I need your help with. My storefront staying closed isn't an issue. In fact, after what happened, I'm not sure I even want to open there again. But my Beverly Hills clients need immediate attention. I'm scheduled to cater a dog's fifth birthday on Friday. I would like you to buy fifty BIS biscuits and a hundred of Tina's special canineolis. Most of my business is in LA, but my e-commerce orders are growing thanks to *Fido's Food Fest*. It's the future, but I can't do it alone. There's enough for every barkery in town."

"You want to share your business with your competitors?"

Talk about a business school no-no. Who did that? You hired more people, rented more space.

"Not exactly. I'm interested in a contract manufacturing agreement. Will you talk to them?"

"I'm not exactly the top dog right now."

Uncle G's roar drowned out Rayelle's laughter. "Out!"

Rayelle didn't flinch as she gestured Bayle to my side. It didn't work. The dog cowered at her feet. I wouldn't want to leave with me either. Uncle G's glare finally did the trick. Bayle looked like a deflated cotton ball as he scurried to my side. I scooped him into my arms and hurried past Uncle G.

"Will you try, Cat?" Rayelle asked.

Rayelle's plea touched me. Of course I would. She'd given me a real reason to visit her competitors. "I can't promise anything, but I'll try." A saleswoman I was not, but sharing the wealth like this could soften the competitive animosity.

"Mind telling me what that was about?" Uncle G inquired.

"Need-to-know," I muttered under my breath as I high-tailed it out of the building. No comment from Uncle G told me he intended to press the info from Rayelle. So, he was protecting her? From what exactly? Need-to-know, Bayle's behind. I'd find out if it killed me.

CHAPTER 7

The block-and-a-half walk from police headquarters to Nell's Sit and Stay Café should've taken five minutes. Bayle's fifteen minute sniff-a-thon tested my patience. What was the deal with him lifting his leg on every tree trunk, light post, and mailbox anyway?

The café occupied a quaint green-gabled craftsman bungalow built in 1921. The wraparound veranda overlooked well-tended gardens overflowing with seasonal daisies and colorful mums. Her holiday decor had a decidedly witchy theme, with pointed, slumped conical hats hanging from the ceiling and cornstalk brooms with fancy holiday bows propped against the wall. Bayle eyed the pair of upright witch's legs sticking out of the lawn but walked by without pause.

If I had any chance of helping Rayelle, the level-headed, business-savvy Nell would be the starting point. Although sisters, Nell and Mel couldn't be more different. While Nell was dark and diplomatic with a lovable lab companion, Mel was a firecracker redhead with a hyperactive Australian Shepherd. I arrived before the lunch rush on purpose. One whiff of browning pastry and rosemary-seasoned chicken and I knew Monday's special was Grandma's Pot Pie.

"I see you have Bayle," Nell remarked.

It was always about the dog. "If you can believe it."

"Good luck with Mr. High Maintenance."

Had to love Bayle's short "Who, me?" bark. "He has some serious health issues," I explained, oddly put out. No one called him a pain but me.

"Really?" Nell motioned for me to sit at the carved oak bar and beckoned a server to bring coffee.

"Better bring the pot," I said, prepared for the worst.

"Do we need Kahlua?"

I chuckled. I couldn't help myself, remembering that all-nighter nursing Nell's aged Labrador Retriever years ago. Maybe my roots did run deeper than the surface gravel in Barkview. "That depends."

Nell waved an employee away. "You have my full attention."

On the spot. I really should've practiced my pitch. "Bayle has pancreatitis." It was odd Gabby hadn't shared that tidbit.

"Oh, you poor baby. No wonder Rayelle won't allow him to eat anything other than her cooking." Soft-hearted Nell stroked Bayle's fluff top. That ham just wiggled in bliss.

"I was just at police..."

"I know. I can't believe Rayelle killed Howard," Nell said. "And you saw the whole thing."

"Not exactly. I just saw the body across the room." The pot shook as I poured two mugs of steaming dark roast. That image would haunt me for a long time. "He was dead when I arrived."

"How is that possible in Barkview?"

My thoughts exactly. I'd always felt so safe here. "I know.

Russ is coming this afternoon..." No sense advertising his role until it was official.

"Say no more. I'll put a meatloaf in the oven. Bet the chief needs comfort food too. But you didn't come here to preorder dinner."

"No, though the dinner special is ideal. Rayelle asked me to talk to you on her behalf."

Wariness I expected, but not a crossed-arm shutout. This rivalry needed to end. "Rayelle would like to buy fifty BIS biscuits for a party she's catering in Beverly Hills. She said she can't let the pups down. Her words, not mine." I mean, really? Who catered a dog's birthday party anyway?

"Beverly Hills, huh?" Was that a stargazed half-smile?

"That's what she said. Most of her business is catering movie sets and parties for famous dogs in Hollywood."

"Famous dogs? Can't be a large market segment," Nell remarked.

"Who knew anyone would have a dog party, never mind cater it?" A dog-dumb comment on my part, judging from Nell's frown. I hurriedly added, "She claims there's more than enough to keep every barkery in Barkview busy."

Contemplative silence I could work with. I sipped my coffee, waiting.

"And she's willing to share?" Nell waited for my nod before adding, "She wants to sell under the Bichon Bisquets brand?"

Trust Nell to get all business on me. I had no idea. Time to improvise. "The brand is well known and successful." Where did this stuff come from? What I knew about balance sheets could fit on a coffee bean.

"What will she pay for the biscuits?"

"Wholesale."

"Twenty-five percent discount."

"Fifty."

Nell chuckled. "She's smart. I'll give her that. You pick up the treats. I'll talk to Mel."

"Tell her to leave the Coke home next time." I shook an imaginary can.

"She didn't…"

"She's on video on Rayelle's front doorstep the night of the murder."

Nell groaned. "I'll talk to her about that, too."

Couldn't ask for more. "By the way, I'm interviewing for a guest chef for next Sunday's show. Interested?"

"Rayelle's idea?" Nell asked.

"Yes." That little lie would be forgiven. "I put the leash in front of the pup hiring her."

"Probably not. Rayelle's great on TV."

More like a natural, given the way the camera loved her.

"But throwing that bone will help public opinion." Nell stood. "I'm a behind-the-scenes kind of gal. Mel, on the other hand, will be a…"

"Challenge." We shared a knowing smile.

"A category-five hurricane." Nell would chat with her about that too. "She didn't kill Howard Looc. She was helping me here."

"I didn't say she did."

"Mel is spirited…"

That had to be the biggest understatement of the year. "What about Michelle?"

"Le Fleur?"

"Why so shocked? Her chamomile biscuits are legendary. The Paris connection will sell well."

Nell giggled. "I thought we were talking about who murdered Howard."

That too. I sipped my coffee without comment, taking a page from Aunt Char's book.

"Fifi in a chef's hat would be worth watching." No hesitation on Michelle's origins. Was Rayelle wrong? I doubted it.

One down. One to go. I packed up Bayle and headed back to my car. Next stop, Ciao Bella Dolce. I considered stopping for a bike helmet, but hey, I wasn't on Tina's radar yet.

CHAPTER 8

Expedience prevailed. I drove west on Oak and parked in my reserved studio spot. Better to walk the three blocks than hunt for beach parking. So, Bayle and I strolled down the boardwalk, admiring the pounding surf and dodging the skateboarders, bicyclists, and rollerbladers on a rare sunny autumn afternoon. Ciao Bella and Ciao Bella Dolce occupied a double lot in tourist central, facing the ocean on the corner of First and Thames Street. From the outdoor patio, there was a romantic view of the historic Victorian Old Barkview Inn and the famous Bark Rock. A Mediterranean color palette and swaying, imported olive trees recreated idyllic Tuscany. Tina's grandparents had opened the restaurant in the 1980s. Tina's mom had taken over after her father's heart attack around 2000. Tina's three brothers had expanded the Ciao Bella franchise, each opening restaurants in the other three corners of San Diego County. Tina and her mother operated the original Ciao Bella Italiano. They'd added the successful barkery, Ciao Bella Dolce, a few years ago.

I approached the black-draped doorway, fully aware of the contrast between Bayle's snow-white fluff and the stark Victorian mourning decor. I carried the dog up the three steps. The aroma of mouth-watering roasted-garlic bread drew me inside the nineteenth-century building, which could have been transplanted from Capalbio in Tuscany. Ceiling murals depicting biblical scenes were framed by rough-hewn wood beams. Majolica pottery added splashes of sunset orange and red to the walls. Colorful harvest pumpkins on straw bales and yellow and gold flowers added to the seasonal feel. Behind the counter, Tina stuffed her signature dog treats, canineolis. Bella, her usually hyperactive Spinone Italiano, lay listlessly at her feet. I could cut the sadness with one of those knives in the butcher block comfortably within her reach.

Dressed head to toe in black except for a red-checkered apron, Tina acknowledged me with a visibly shaky nod.

"I-I'm so sorry, Tina."

Tina dabbed her red-rimmed eyes with a shredded tissue. "I loved him. He was a difficult man. Though not like my dad," she added quickly.

Although he'd passed long before I arrived in Barkview, Joseph Principato's overbearing, macho-man persona was still discussed. Then the memory of my dad's funeral hit me like a brick to the back of the head. I must've squeezed Bayle because he whimpered. "It's okay to mourn," I said. "You know, you could close the restaurant. Everyone will understand."

"No!" A spark of her fierce self flared and was extinguished. "I need to keep busy. The kids are home with Mama. Joey understands Howard is in heaven, but it hasn't sunk in yet. Bianca just asks for him."

At ages nine and seven, they would understand soon enough. "Did Howard see them every day?"

She nodded. "He was a good father. The kids were his life." The filling squirted out of the pastry gun onto the counter, the same shape and color as the doggie doo I'd stepped in at Rayelle's. Prank solved. No wonder Bayle ate it up. Was that only sixteen hours ago?

"Thank you for the flowers. They are beautiful."

I nodded. "Anything I can do to help?" Thank goodness Aunt Char never missed a beat. I hadn't even thought about flowers yet.

"Where is Bolt? I forgot to ask the chief," Tina said.

"I don't know." The dog had cut his head when he broke through the car window. "I'll find him."

"*Grazie. Mio caro* dreamed of winning the national flyball trophy. I must do it for him."

All Howard's business and patent interests and his wife thought his legacy should be a trophy in a dog game? No wonder she wanted Bolt back. "Uh, I'll come back."

"No. It's okay. Why did you come?"

I eyed the knives within Tina's reach. I'd promised. "Rayelle asked me to talk to you."

Tina stiffened, her glare focused on Bayle. "That dog ruined my life."

"I don't understand." Clearly, Tina thought there was more to Rayelle and Howard's relationship than Rayelle admitted, too.

Her finger shake, directed at Bayle, was all Italian. "Bella was out the moment he came to town." On cue, Bella growled. Bayle jerked back, butting into my chin.

I spat white fur out of my mouth for the umpteenth time. "That's why you joined Sean Riley's team."

"Of course. Howard forced me to." Tina wiped her hands on her apron and stroked Bella from head to tail.

In retrospect, Tina running to Howard's rival to retaliate

made too much sense. The man had replaced his wife's dog with a younger woman's. Classic motive for murder with a Barkview twist? Although Uncle G had confirmed Tina's alibi, I suddenly wasn't so sure.

I glanced from the knife block to the plate stack and the exit, confirming my exit strategy. "Uh, did Howard mention divorce?"

Her look slayed without a knife in hand. I gulped.

"Gabby has a big mouth."

Better Gabby than me on Tina's radar. I nodded in what I hoped passed as sympathetic agreement.

Tina spoke through pressed lips. "Howard came by to pick up Joey right after I'd hung up with Gabby. I asked him point-blank. He gave me his quirky grin and told me all in good time."

Serious Howard had a quirky grin? "What does that mean?"

"He didn't want a divorce. Something was going on. He wouldn't tell me what, which wasn't unusual. He always had something going on. I stopped trying to keep up." More tears. "Now, it's too late."

I felt like a jerk. Who questioned a widow fifteen hours after her husband's murder? "Uh, as I said, I came to talk to you on Rayelle's behalf."

Tina straightened to her full five-foot-six height. "I do not forgive her."

"Okay. She wants to buy one hundred of your special canineolis for a catering job in Hollywood on Thursday." I bit back my smile as Tina's jaw dropped.

"She is willing to help me?"

Did Tina need help? She'd always seemed so self-sufficient. "If you promise not to leave your canineoli filling on her doorstep anymore, she'll help you a whole lot more."

Did Tina's arched brows express surprise or acquiescence? "I'm not a charity case for a guilty conscience."

"She'll pay wholesale. Rayelle's main business is catering Hollywood dog events."

Tina took a double-take. "Hollywood. Like for Marley?"

"Who?"

"You know, the lab from the movie *Marley & Me*?"

I stared. What could I say?

"Jennifer Aniston and Owen Wilson starred in the movie about..."

"I know the movie. That had to be ten years ago. Is Marley even still alive?" Of all the famous dogs on TV to choose.

"It's not important. So, that's her secret." The eye of a hurricane came to mind, the calm before the crazy wind. Even Bella stepped back. Bayle nudged me toward the door. I guess it's true. Dogs do have a self-preservationist sixth sense. I should run, not walk, away.

Did Tina watch *Fido's Food Fest*? We'd talked about catering before. "Think about it and let me know." I inched toward the door. Not fast enough. Before I could escape, Tina's diminutive grandmother commanded the room with a shaking floured rolling pin. "No help that...ladra." Dressed entirely in black, with only a thin band on her ring finger, a lifetime creating Italian masterpieces had not ruined Nonna's slim figure.

Hands on her hips, Tina met her grandmother straight on. "She will pay us to make one hundred canineolis for a rich dog's party."

The rolling pin paused mid-arc. "One hundred?"

I sensed my escape. "Uh, I'll let you two work this out." My butt bumped a wood table as I inched toward the exit. Bayle's full body shiver diminished his growl.

"We'll do it," Tina shouted.

Goal accomplished, I cocooned Bayle in my arms and high-tailed it to freedom, the door closing behind me with a bang. Bayle's frantic heartbeat matched mine for a few blocks before his weight caused me to put him down as I speed-walked back to the KDOG studio. Tina's grief had been genuine. Her alliance with J. Tracker's owner, Sean Riley, suddenly brought a new interpretation to the documents I'd found in Howard's briefcase. The men's rivalry hadn't ended there.

I met Aunt Char in the parking lot. Dressed in cream slacks and an aqua hunt scene blouse with a coordinating scarf, she looked as fresh and elegant as usual. Why couldn't I have inherited any of her style? I had the girl next door covered down to the broken-in jeans and blotchy lipstick in desperate need of reapplication. "What are you doing here so early?"

"Hello, Bayle." Aunt Char crouched to dog level. Bayle trotted into her hug, his tongue a pink flash against her cheek. Yuck.

Aunt Char stroked Bayle. "Tina called. Sean has offered to buy Howard's company, Petronics."

"Already? Howard hasn't been dead for twenty-four hours."

"It is in poor taste."

"And suspect." Why hadn't Tina said anything to me? "Why did she call you?"

Aunt Char's shrug didn't reassure me. I crossed my arms and waited. "Legally, I am the managing partner of Petronics now."

Oh, no. Following the money led straight to my aunt. "Last time we talked about Petronics, you'd donated money on behalf of the shelter."

"Originally, it was a loan, but in August Howard insisted I buy twenty-five percent of Petronics stock. Our ownership agreement gives me administrative control of the company."

"Twenty-five percent is a minority stake."

"Yes. Tina and Howard's two children inherited twenty-five percent each. Howard insisted if something happened to him that I become the custodian of his children's inheritance until they turn twenty-five." In eighteen years she'd be free.

"Tina inherits the remaining twenty-five percent."

"No. Alan Thorpe, Petronics general manager and CFO, retains ten percent. Tina is a fifteen percent stakeholder."

She had to be furious.

"I have first right of refusal to buy out the company at market value. Howard insisted on assurances that his chip was developed properly."

A serious motive for Aunt Char. I couldn't even think about the possible ramifications for the mayoral race yet. First I had to make sure she wasn't a suspect.

"Why does Alan Thorpe have a stake?" I asked.

"It's not unusual to offer ownership to attract top talent for a start-up."

"Did Howard make the changes after Tina joined J. Tracker's flyball team?"

"I never really connected that, but yes."

"Tina wants to sell." I already knew that. Howard knew Sean all too well.

"She asked me to consider it. Tina Looc is no fool. J. Tracker is an excellent candidate to develop the chip technology."

Or steal it back? "No offense, Aunt Char, you're a good manager, but why Howard's sudden interest in finding someone else to run the company?"

"It wasn't exactly sudden. He'd asked me to partner with him when he founded Petronics. I agreed this time to protect his children."

Aunt Char's efforts to protect animals and children were legendary. "Does Sean know you stand between him and

Howard's technology?" If Sean had thought Tina would inherit the business upon Howard's death...

"Yes. Tina told him this morning."

Great. Did that put Aunt Char in possible danger? "How did he take it?"

"He chuckled."

"What?" Who laughed about a plan foiled?

"Don't read too much into it. I imagine Sean believes I will sell if the offer is right."

"Sell to Howard's nemesis? He'll haunt you forever."

Aunt Char shivered. "Howard trusted me to protect his children's interests."

At the cost of his own? "You think Howard would want Sean to get control of his invention again?"

Point made, based on the twin creases marring Aunt Char's brow. "There's more to it than that. My information is telling me J. Tracker is not as financially sound as it could be."

"A result of the Cavalier kidnappings?" I asked.

"The dognappings renewed interest in injectable trackers like Howard's."

"So, he needs the new technology to survive?"

"I imagine it's not that severe, but a new product in the pipeline will certainly be beneficial." She stopped further conjecture with a forefinger wave. "I will reserve judgment until I understand the recent product settlement. That information will be in Howard's files. I'm on my way there now."

"I'm coming with you."

"I thought you might. I imagine this doesn't look good for me either."

"Not to mention your mayoral campaign," I had to add.

"Life does have a way of reprioritizing." I'd expected more than a shrug from my aunt after her months of endless politicking.

"Do you know who F. Hazing is?" I asked.

"No."

I checked my watch. "I need to see Stephan and Stephanie. I'll meet you at Petronics. Russ will be here in a few hours."

No sneaking that bit of info by. Aunt Char's "I see" spoke volumes I'd refused to consider earlier. "The chief asked him to assist in finding Howard's murderer."

"Then he's the best man for the job."

"So Uncle G says."

"Yet you are still suspicious?"

I couldn't meet her gaze.

"Russ will prove Rayelle's innocence."

I knew that. Why did I think this was one big conspiracy?

"You haven't come to terms with the secretive nature of his job, have you?" Aunt Char asked.

"I have a fundamental problem with secrets." I felt compelled to uncover them.

"Perhaps Russ being in Barkview is too close to home."

I hated it when she drilled down to the real truth. "Physically or emotionally?"

"Do you feel like he's invading your space?" Aunt Char asked.

I wanted to deny it, but... "Maybe."

"Perhaps you should ask yourself if you're ready for the next step in this relationship."

"It's not that." Or was it? I jerked my finger through my bangs. "It's just a weird feeling. I mean, what if he is already involved in this case somehow?"

She squeezed my hand. "He will first and foremost protect you."

Yes. He would. The man was a real live knight in shining armor. The warm and fuzzy didn't last, though. "Not knowing is not protecting me."

"Some say it's bliss," Aunt Char remarked.

Not to me. Good, bad, or ugly, I dealt with the truth. I took no comfort from her hug. Was Howard somehow on the FBI's radar? Just thinking about it made my head pound. So did challenging the delicate trust bond between Russ and me so soon.

CHAPTER 9

Beach parking being at a premium, I half-dragged the meandering sniff-monster the two blocks to the Frosty Pups Creamery. The 1922 beach bungalow, originally built as a rumrunner's lookout, enjoyed a colorful past that included serving as an early-warning radar station during World War II and a surfer's hostel in the 1960s and 1970s. Five years ago, Stephan and Stephanie McCarthy had pooled their inheritances and restored the Craftsman building, complete with a shore rock chimney and paned bay windows.

Fitting with the ghost tour theme, fog-shrouded gravestones lined the shell path to the creamery. Inside, acrylic block-like tables and cube chairs sat in front of smoked-glass windows in what I called a Scandinavian minimalist style. White molding framed sky-blue walls accented with glass-mounted dog silhouettes draped with spider webs that did not invite lingering. Spirits levitated above the room, watching my every move.

BB, Stephanie's Blue Bay Shepherd, loped across the black-and-white checkerboard floor, blocking my entry while

Bayle, the great protector, growled from behind the safety of my legs.

"Bayle's helpful." Stephanie stashed a Mr. Clean spray bottle and rag behind the counter. Except for her sunburn-prone complexion, Stephanie looked anything but Irish, with her French-braided, blue-black hair.

Blockaded by an eighty-pound Blue Bay German Shepherd, I had no choice but to pause. "Walmart's got your greeter beat."

"Don't count on it. BB, bow." The dog's black head dipped in regal regard.

"Impressive."

Stephanie's smile released the tension. "BB, sit." The dog obeyed, her silver-blue coat blending as one with her lab coat. The canine-human resemblance even included matching sky-blue eyes. "Why are you here?"

"For the yogurt." I looped Bayle's leash over my wrist and strolled to the gleaming bank of self-serve yogurt machines. Naturally, Bayle had other plans and jerked me toward the Pups Cream dispensers. My paper cup launched into the air.

Like a star third baseman, Stephanie snatched the cup midair. "Do you want me to take Bayle or get your yogurt?"

Much as I liked to create my own culinary masterpiece, I could have sworn BB's lip-licking grin had Bayle-snack written all over it. As a dog protector, I had to be the joke of the century. Resigned, I said, "Triple dark chocolate yogurt and pineapple with fresh strawberries, blueberries, coconut, and chocolate chunks, please."

Stephanie didn't bother to hide her chuckle. "You're a wimp letting that dog get away with bad behavior, but a good friend. Hope Rayelle appreciates that."

Me too. I plopped down on a hard plastic box and watched Stephanie dish up my lunch. "Anything for Bayle?" she asked.

"Can't. He has pancreatitis." I watched her response.

Her dark brows arched. "Well. That explains it."

Apparently, it did. From exasperation to eye-widening understanding in four words. Why had Rayelle kept Bayle's health condition secret?

Stephanie delivered my treat and scratched Bayle's fluffy head. He just stood there quietly taking it all in.

"If only he'd be so well behaved for me." I dipped the blue spoon into the rich probiotic chocolate.

"No love for the surrogate," Stephanie remarked.

All of the responsibility and none of the loyalty. I was okay with that, I reminded myself, as the bittersweet chocolate melted on my tongue, energizing me. Yummy. Best lunch ever.

"Why are you here?" Stephanie asked.

I savored another spoonful. As if she didn't know. "Rayelle installed cameras last night at Bichon Bisquets. They caught BB dropping an envelope on the doorstep around eleven."

"Impossible. BB, Stephan, and I closed last night. We didn't get out of here until after midnight, when I saw you at the murder scene." Her ocean-blue manicured nails peeked through BB's long hair. "Other than a piece of my mind, what could I possibly want to give Rayelle?"

"A defamation lawsuit."

"There's an idea."

As if savvy Stephanie hadn't considered that.

"Seriously, I couldn't care less what she says about my peanut butter and carrot Pups Cream. Dogs love it, and that's what matters to me."

BB's tongue slipped in and out again, just daring me to contradict that truth. I took a long, critical look at the dog. Did her lupine features seem less pointed than the dog on the video? Her bluish-gray fur did appear to be bluer than black and lighter than the grainy images from Rayelle's camera.

"Mind if I take a profile shot of BB?" Better to compare the two images side by side.

"'Course not." Stephanie's quick agreement should've indicated she had nothing to hide.

BB posed like a hunting lodge statue. I snapped two pictures. "How well did you know Howard Looc?"

She shrugged. "Howard was no surfer."

True. He was more like a cerebral nerd. Talk about Stephan's polar opposite. "Is your brother around?"

Stephanie's ice-blue glare turned glacial and froze Bayle's fidgeting.

"He'll be around soon. Graveyards and Ghosts is busy at this time of the year."

No doubt. "I understand he and Tina were involved."

Was her chuckle forced? "That's old news."

"I hear they're talking again."

"Stephan is mourning Thunder. Tina chose that pup for him. Best thing she ever did."

That explained nothing. "What really happened between them?"

"Trite as it sounds, Howard swept Tina off her feet. My brother got dissed."

"Bad breakup?"

Stephanie's "Uh-huh" held no small degree of animosity. "If you're looking for a suspect, Tina had the most to gain by Howard's death."

I scraped the yogurt bowl for the last spoonful. "The spouse is always a suspect." I didn't add she had an airtight alibi. Better to let Stephanie talk.

"Turns out she married a control freak just like her father."

Howard? "First I've heard Howard called that."

"In public he put on the lovey-dovey act. In private..."

I leaned in so as not to miss a word.

"Tina and Bolt joined BB and me for a Frisbee toss back in March. When Tina threw one for Bolt, the wonder dog just stared at her. Even after some coaching, he couldn't catch the Frisbee. Howard found us an hour later, and he totally lost it. I mean, Tina was a paddlepuss."

"A what?" Surfing lingo wasn't exactly intuitive.

"That's a dudette who only plays in the whitewater."

"You mean she didn't argue with him?" I asked.

"Yeah. I didn't believe Stephan's stories about Howard until I saw the behavior in person. Howard was outta control."

A control freak with a temper hardly fit what I knew about methodical Howard Looc. "Did Tina throw a plate at him?"

"The knife incident happened a week later." Stephanie scratched BB. "Ever wonder why Tina doesn't have a lot of friends?"

Between caring for two young children, running a successful restaurant and barkery, and competing in flyball, I'd say time constraints.

"Howard monitored who she saw and where she went."

A *putter-putter* and then a gunshot/backfire sound made Stephanie and me jump in unison. No confusing that sound with a Vespa. "Stephan's here. I keep telling him to dump that piece of junk," Stephanie said as her brother strolled in.

"Chill, sis. Can't you just feel the vibe of Gran and Gramps hanging ten at Huntington in this bug?" A male version of his sister, Stephan's black hair skimmed his shoulders. Instead of a neat lab coat, he wore an Old West undertaker's coat and stovepipe hat. His striking pale blue eyes were ringed in day-of-the-dead black.

"Cat wants to know about you and Tina," Stephanie announced. "I told her about Howard."

"Howard moved to the casino six months ago. Surely, she..." I said.

"Was starting to feel safe." Stephan's pressed lips dared Stephanie to disagree.

"She said she was afraid of Howard?" I asked.

Stephan scratched his scruffy beard. "Not exactly afraid. She said he was more like her dad than she'd thought."

"In what way?"

"Just that he wanted to control her."

From soul mates to a control freak, what was the real story behind the Loocs' relationship? "You spoke with her often?" I asked.

"Not really. I thought she'd want to know when my dog, Thunder, died."

"Did she?"

His wistful smile said more than his words. "I miss her."

"The dog," Stephanie clarified. "Not the murder victim's wife."

Stephan shook off what looked like a trip down memory lane. "Right. Tina's just a friend."

Not sure who he was trying to convince there.

"Steph's helper was a no-show to close Sunday night. My last tour ended at nine, I went to play darts, but Steph needed my help so I came back. The shop closed at eleven. We wiped down the dispensers after closing, until midnight." Stephan flicked a cobweb off his sleeve. "Didn't get outta here until we heard the sirens."

It all sounded too reasonable and rehearsed. No cameras at the Frosty Pups meant no confirmations either. My gut didn't have an opinion. "You are Barkview's resident ghost expert. What do you know about the Vespa Guardian?"

I swear Stephanie paled. Stephan shared a look with his sister, one of those twin things I'd read about. "Folks report a noise like a Vespa and a ghostly apparition," Stephan answered.

"Don't forget the orange eyes," Stephanie added.

"You've seen it?" Gabby I could buy, but levelheaded Stephanie?

"Only from a distance. It was enough."

Stephanie's apprehension seemed real. She'd seen something. So much for thinking they'd made the whole thing up. I focused on Stephan. "What about you?"

"Nope," Stephan said.

"You never missed curfew?" Hard to believe Stephanie was the only curfew breaker in the family.

"Nope."

There had to be more. Stephanie cleared it up. "Tina's three older brothers were scarier than any ghost."

Never underestimate familial fear. "So, what's the story on the ghost?" Every ghost had to have a story, right?

"No one really knows. The ghost hangs around the Barkview parking spots. Comes out on waxing and sliver moons. Cruises the dogwood and Bark Rock lookout. If Steph hadn't seen it, I'd have sworn our parents made it up," Stephan insisted.

I wanted to believe him. "I'm not going to find a black Vespa with orange lights and a metallic cape in your shop am I?"

"No." Stephan seemed offended. "G&G Tours only uses fat-tire electric scooters." He read my confusion. "The scooters don't make noise."

Stephan pulled up his starched collar. In a sinister voice, he said, "Barkview has many skeletons that are better kept hidden. Look too deeply and you will never be the same."

Theatrics aside, what exactly did he know? Did he think he could deter me with a veiled warning? Might as well wave a red cape. Secrets needed to be uncovered.

CHAPTER 10

J. Tracker's larger-than-life Jack Russell head perched atop their smoked-glass world headquarters stared down at me as I drove into the Barkview Industrial Complex. The hillside acreage located on the east side of Interstate 5 had an abundance of stately Torrey pines that had dictated the twists and turns in the road.

Nearly blinded by the afternoon sun, I dropped the driver's side visor as I zigzagged past several buildings before parking beside Aunt Char's Mercedes in front of Petronics' nothing-but-business concrete structure with few windows. I hadn't connected just how different Howard and Sean were until that moment.

Bayle mush-dogged me to the glass entry door beneath a discreet Petronics sign and a single Halloween jack-o'-lantern. I'd bet even money Bayle had been here before.

Entering the building required scanning both my finger-prints and ID before Aunt Char could buzz me in. The security overkill here, compared to J. Tracker's lone receptionist and cameras, bothered me. Did Howard have cause to be paranoid? Industrial espionage wasn't generally a crime of opportunity.

I walked into a stark, Scandinavian-modern reception area. A vacant gray workstation protected a corridor lined with flyball photos. Four steps down the hall, I tripped over Bayle, who whined and stood ready to chase.

A corridor somehow meant ball retrieval. How had I put that one together? I patted my pants pockets and then glanced in my shoulder bag. Wallet, keys, mirror. No ball. "Sorry, boy. I'll do better next time."

Bayle wasn't buying it. He darted around and around my feet, bouncing off my shins as he mummified my legs with his leash, barking a rant. Yikes. My misbehaving-dog tolerance was about to end. A four-year-old behaved better.

A single, decisive bark shattered the chaos and froze everything—a bark I knew, even before Renny's single perfect Cavalier spotted head peeked out of a distant doorway. Bayle's tirade ended with a pathetic whimper. He dropped to his stomach, all four legs grounded.

Renny's head toss reprimanded me. Give me a break. I was the injured party, the one about to keel over which was likely her point. Until Rayelle claimed him, responsibility for Bayle's behavior fell to me.

Just great. What I knew about dog discipline amounted to zero. I unwound my legs. No need to reprimand him further. In her queenly manner, Renny had cowed him good.

I scooped up the quivering fluff-ball and followed Renny into what had to be Howard's office. The minimalist decor continued inside with a modern desk and leather chairs. Only ceiling-high potted bamboo plants offered any warmth, although the pots' ceramic design depicted a bloody, horse-mounted battle. Not a dog in sight, but they were not forgotten. A large doggie door led into a Zen garden. Granted, I was accustomed to Cavalier-sized doggie-doors, but that door looked like I could fit through it.

Bayle squirmed out of my grip and barked a single throw-the-ball bark. Obsessed hardly seemed an adequate tag. Not a minute ago he'd been barked into submission.

No wonder Renny lunged, but no Barkview Cavalier was going to behave so disrespectfully around Aunt Char. She caught Renny with her right hand. She felt around the pile of papers on the desktop with her left and tossed a red ball across the room. In a white cloud, Bayle bounded after it. I plopped into the stiff chair.

"That dog needs discipline." I expected agreement, not my aunt's indulgent smile.

"Give the poor dear a break."

I shared a shudder with Renny. "He's driving me crazy."

"He's just testing you."

A dog test? "I thought a dog's main goal was to make people happy."

"Their masters, yes. You have taken Rayelle away from him. He's acting out."

"Dog psychology 101?" My head pounded.

"Bayle doesn't understand your limits yet. You are not communicating with him."

"Me? I'm…" I couldn't be controlled by a twenty-four-pound puff. I refused to allow it.

Aunt Char continued, "Think of yourself as the substitute teacher. He will try to get away with whatever you let him. A firm no and he will learn."

Bayle dropped the ball at my feet. I threw it down the long hall, watching him rabbit-hop after it. I swear Renny's gaze said, "I told you so."

"Can Renny help me control him?"

"And deprive you of this life lesson?"

I clenched my jaw. "Life lesson?"

My aunt's laugh didn't bode well for me. "Getting along with others."

"I get along with Renny." I didn't need to see Renny's unblinking gaze to remind me how fiery that relationship had been.

"Here's the time I point out that every breed has different characteristics." Aunt Char scratched Renny's ear.

I wasn't jealous. Okay, maybe a little. Those two belonged together. "I know, but the basics should be the same."

My aunt's eye roll said otherwise. "What worked with Renny will likely not with Bayle. Bichons are more active. Not Jack Russell active, but more than a Cavalier. Bayle will happily sit on the couch with you after he's used up some energy."

"So I throw the ball." It wasn't really a question, but rather acceptance. My mood did not improve with Aunt Char's nod. This sounded like me adapting to a dog, again.

On cue, Bayle bounded into the room, the red ball poking out of his mouth. He dropped the ball at my feet, his tail dusting my shin in swift swings. I threw the ball again.

Time to change the subject. "Do you intend to run Petronics now?"

"Howard's general manager, Alan Thorpe, will continue to run day-to-day operations. Alan's Golden Retriever is also on Howard's flyball team."

By design or chance? I made a note to talk to him on my ever-ready Post-its with the chief's pen. Apparently, "thief" did apply here. "How involved was Howard in operations?"

"We will find out." I caught Aunt Char's ghost of a smile. "Howard also left me a letter." She adjusted her reading glasses.

If you are reading this I did not anticipate all outcomes. I trust you will care for my wife and children. Execute the chip technology rollout as outlined within. Trust the chief to appoint the proper lieutenants. Protect yours, dear Charlotte. Never lose sight of what is important.

Aunt Char never did. Howard Looc had appointed the right guardian for the children's business interests. His words also opened a window into his world. And birthed a million questions Uncle G could likely answer if he chose.

My aunt waved a fistful of legal documents. "These are the J. Tracker settlement papers. Howard left them in his top drawer."

"That's strange."

"I'm not sure. He could have simply been reviewing them. The settlement was straightforward. J. Tracker paid Howard five-point-five million dollars for his share of the J. Tracker collar patent royalties. Howard waived his right to future royalties. No restrictions were placed on Petronics' current collar or technology Howard had developed while employed by J. Tracker." Aunt Char frowned. "Reading between the lines, I would guess Howard did play a bigger part in inventing the technology than Sean admits."

I crushed another Post-it into my pocket. "Why would Howard forfeit future royalties?"

"He believed the injectable was the future."

"So, what's bothering you?"

"Exactly why Howard wanted me involved."

Good question. "Marketing? Your endorsement will launch the project."

Aunt Char blushed. "My influence isn't that extensive."

"Oh, but it is. Coupled with your celebrity and the Barklay Kennel's reputation, the injectable will be an instant success." I glanced at Renny sitting sphinxlike by Aunt Char's feet.

"The dog world is small…"

"More like incestuous." That one slipped out. "I meant everyone knows everybody."

"Well, yes. Show dogs are a limited market."

She had a point. "How much will the chip sell for at retail? I thought you said it would be used for rescues."

"Only if it can be mass-produced. Currently, injectable technology is price prohibitive. Howard wanted to meet on Friday. He said he had an idea he wanted to discuss with me."

"Can F. Hazing help?" I asked on a whim.

Aunt Char's double take offered little hope. I removed the drawings from my tote and laid them on the desk. I dreaded telling her where I got them, but she needed to know.

"This looks like the chip drawing." Aunt Char adjusted her reading glasses. "What are the peaks above the Petronics logo?"

"JRu's ears."

It took a second to connect the dots, but Aunt Char's gape was priceless.

"Someone covered J. Tracker's logo with Petronics' logo," I said.

"And you think this is intellectual property theft? But how did you…?" She held up her hand. "Never mind. I don't want to know. Unlike you, I find ignorance restive."

That dig hit home. Why did I always need answers? Because deep down I was a reporter driven by curiosity. Or was it fear of the unknown?

No censure from Aunt Char, just a sudden weariness as she methodically removed her glasses. "Unfortunately, now that I am aware of potential wrongdoing, I am honor bound to investigate."

Renny's head rose as if cued. No way she'd understood. Yet her unblinking stare followed Aunt Char across the room to a pen-and-ink drawing of an egret above the wall table. She slid the picture aside and pressed her hand on the scanner. The safe's door clicked open. She sorted through a file stack, selected one, and then brought it to the desk. I scooted to her side of the desk as she laid the Petronics drawings side by side with mine.

"For the record, I do not believe Howard would do anything illegal without a good reason."

That was telling. "You're talking about the dangers of rivalries."

"Howard was grounded. Comfortable with his accomplishments. And a first-class strategist."

"He had faults. Ask Tina."

"I wonder about that."

"What does that mean?"

"Tina was the love of his life. I've often wondered if he pushed her away to protect her from something," Aunt Char said.

It was my turn to just listen as Aunt Char continued. "Howard initiated the separation for no apparent reason. His greatest joy was his children. Yet, six months ago he moved into a hotel."

Her assessment of Howard sounded shockingly similar to Uncle G's. "I'm surprised Howard didn't mention Bolt in his wishes. Tina told me she wants him," I said.

"Bolt is part of the Looc family. There's more." Aunt Char leaned back in the desk chair and exhaled. I really wasn't going to like what she had to say next. "Howard left the rights to his flyball team's name to Alan and Bolt's offspring to Rayelle."

Red flags popped up everywhere. Alan managed the flyball team. His ownership made some sense. But Rayelle, a mere business associate, potentially controlling the future of

Howard's greatest possession? "I don't understand. Bolt has puppies?"

"Apparently, Bolt was bred with a champion Border Collie. The puppies are due next month. The sire gets the pick of the litter."

"Which may or may not be something." How many Cavalier puppies had Aunt Char groomed to show that ended up as pampered pets?

"True. Question is, why? The way Rayelle tells it, she's only just committed to Bayle playing on Howard's team."

"Does Tina know?" If not, the plate casualties promised to be exponential.

"Not unless Howard told her. I just noted the change in his living trust forty-four days ago."

That coincided with Rayelle's relocation. It still didn't prove Rayelle killed Howard, but it did add more doubt.

"I didn't realize you knew Howard so well," I remarked.

"JB played cards with him."

"And Uncle G." Now I remembered the never-a-dull-moment Texas Hold'em nights with Aunt Char's late husband during my dog attack recovery. "Doesn't Howard have—didn't he have—a photographic memory?"

"Eidetic memory."

"Isn't that cheating?"

Aunt Char chuckled. "JB never tired of teasing him about it. He enjoyed beating Howard."

"Who was the fourth player?"

"Sean Riley's father."

Sean must've loved that.

"Howard was so supportive after JB's death. I couldn't turn down his request to oversee his children's financial future."

Who would've thought my aunt would have to execute last

wishes for a man in his forties? "What do you think Howard was involved in?" I asked.

"I don't know exactly. I do know that above all Howard would protect his family."

With that in mind, Uncle G's behavior made more sense. Not why he tasked Russ with this investigation, but why he defended Howard. What could an ingenious inventor and Uncle G be involved in that could lead to murder?

CHAPTER 11

The biggest issue with living at the beach had to be parking. I had a garage, but visitors needed more than a fair bit of luck to find a space anywhere. When I found my assistant, Sandy, blocking my driveway, I should've known it had to do with my charge. Bayle recognized the angled flyball launcher Sandy carried inside before I did. He beelined to Sandy, ripping the leash out of my hand as he ran figure eights through her legs, power-barking.

"Wow, boy. Calm down." How Sandy avoided Bayle's sensitive paws while balancing the awkward board had to be a testament to agility. Disaster loomed, mostly for my walls.

"Bayle, sit," I commanded. The dog acknowledged nothing, continuing his leg attack and ear-piercing barking. I tried again. Louder this time, as if I meant it. "Sit!"

His head cocked my way. I had his attention. Indecision flickered in those Belgian-chocolate eyes. No way I'd lose now. I pointed to the ground. "Sit!" My follow-up worked. His butt hit the tile floor, his tail still dusting expectantly.

"Give him a treat," Sandy urged me.

"For what? Not tripping you? Isn't that rewarding bad behavior?"

"He obeyed your command. Give him a treat. This dog is ball and treat motivated, remember?"

How could I forget? I patted my pockets. No treat.

I didn't need to see Sandy's eye roll to recognize her exasperation. "The green container on your counter. Hurry, or you'll miss your chance."

I sprinted to the kitchen and returned with a handful of heart-shaped cookies. Trust Rayelle to bake them with love. Bayle tongue-snatched the treat out of my hand while I squeezed the rest between the Post-its in my pockets. "Stay." I offered him a second reward. Remarkably, the tornado sat still. His leg quiver told me he wanted to attack the board, but he stayed as directed.

Sandy released him the moment she set the board at the far end of the hallway. "Go."

Bayle took off like a sprinter in the blocks, just about flying across the tile. His front paws landed on the ball launcher and a red ball arched upward. The dog caught it midair, pivoted, and sprinted back at me. I hopped aside, sure I'd get rammed. He dropped the ball at my feet and whirled around, ready for another run.

"Woo! He is fast," Sandy remarked. "No wonder Howard lobbied for him to join his team."

No kidding. "Bayle replaced Bella."

Sandy's whistle resonated. "Double-dumb move, Mr. Looc. Goes to show you IQ isn't a prereq for marital bliss."

Part of me wanted to agree, but Aunt Char's insightful look into Howard did make me question his motives. Had Howard intentionally replaced his wife's dog to end their marriage? The supposed master strategist had to have anticipated she would overreact. Maybe not run to his nemesis, but do something over the top.

Bayle retrieved four balls before plopping down at my feet, panting. Even I recognized the expectant cock of his head. I offered him another treat. He gobbled it, keeping Sandy in view as she reloaded the balls. I expected him to resume the game. Instead, he trotted to his food bowl. Another aha moment for me. I quickly removed his pre-made food from the fridge and spooned it into his dish. I swear he smiled at me as he wolfed it down. A few minutes later, a red ball in his mouth, he moseyed to the window seat and curled up for a snooze.

"Quick bursts of energy followed by, in this case, eating." Sandy's reminder helped me find perspective.

I pointed to the board. "How did you know?"

Sandy laughed. "Rayelle figured you'd be ready to kill him about now."

Rayelle knew her dog and me. "He's a more active dog than a Cavalier. Not hard, just different. Rayelle suggested I get it. She asked the chief for clothes, too."

Had to be good news that she hadn't been issued that county jumpsuit yet.

"She told the chief you desperately needed the flyball machine. Emphasis on 'desperately.' The chief had Officer Richie escort me to Bichon Bisquets." Sandy looked over both shoulders and whispered, "I couldn't find the envelope we saw on Rayelle's surveillance tape. The chief must have it."

Now everything made sense. Trust Sandy to use an opportunity for evidence retrieval. "I worked on the video's graininess and I'm not sure it was Stephanie's dog anyway. Seriously, the dog kind of looked like a Timber Wolf."

"A Timber Wolf?"

"Yeah. I volunteered at Wolf Rescue a few years ago. From a

distance they resemble a German Shepherd. Up close, their faces are more angular."

I believed her. Sandy loved all animals, big and small. "Not a good fit for me," she admitted.

Silence seemed prudent. What could I say, anyway?

"If I'm right, that was a well-trained wolf," Sandy remarked.

"Are there wolf-dog mixes?"

"It's illegal to own a wolf in the United States. In California, if the dog is fifty percent wolf, you need a permit from Fish and Game. There aren't any in Barkview. I checked. The dog has to be handled as an exotic animal. They make vicious guard dogs."

I twisted my scarf. Couldn't help myself. Big dog bicuspids always made my bite-scar sting.

"Sorry. I saw Russ at the police station. Rumor has it..."

"He's assisting in the investigation," I finished for her.

"How, uh, do you feel about that?" Not as smooth as Aunt Char's personal probing, but equally as effective.

"I'm not sure." Which was more or less true. I owed him a chance to explain. The clock striking the half hour meant avoidance wouldn't last much longer either.

"He's not a bad choice," Sandy said diplomatically. "He's got Barkview wired and he has worked a case here before..." Sandy's arched brow indicated more. She stopped my questioning by saying, "He'll prove Rayelle's innocence if she didn't do it."

"You doubt her?" Was I reading too much into Sandy's word choice or had her full support wavered?

"The evidence is..."

"Circumstantial." I said. Just wait until I told her about Bolt's puppies and the flyball team.

"Mounting." Sandy's precise pronunciation concerned me.

"The latest is that Howard has forgiven Rayelle's rent since she moved in."

Gabby wasted no time broadcasting that info. "It's not unheard of for a landlord to give incentives to a new business."

"Not when they're already charging half the going rate in a full occupancy zone."

"A flyball bribe?"

"If Rayelle is to be believed," Sandy said.

Was I blind? I'd been wrong before. "You don't believe Rayelle?"

"She's not telling the whole story. I'm afraid of what will come out next," Sandy explained.

Part of me agreed. "Does the chief see the free rent as a bribe?"

"More like evidence of a deeper relationship." Sandy scratched her chin. "Thing is, he's hiding something, too."

"No doubt. But what?"

Sandy's ponytail swing offered no insight. We'd have to keep digging. Time to exit save-Rayelle mode and investigate like the reporter I'd trained to be. "Do you know Alan Thorpe?"

"His Golden Retriever is a champion flyballer on Howard's team."

Sandy really did know everything. "Was he Howard's GM before or after his dog joined Howard's team?" Establishing a pattern always helped understanding.

"I'll find out. I'll also check into his history."

"Did you know Stephan and Tina were an item?"

"In high school. That's old news."

"They've been talking again."

"That's interesting."

I had Sandy's full attention. "Can you find out who closes at the Frosty Pups Creamery on Sunday night?"

"I think so. Why?"

"Stephanie made sure I knew Stephan was with her all evening the night Howard died."

"And you think..."

"I wonder why she felt compelled to do it."

"I'll find the usual closer and talk to him or her," Sandy promised.

"Stephanie also painted a picture of Howard dominating Tina."

Laughter spilled from Sandy's lips. "Nerdy Howard bossing Tina around?"

"I know. It seems crazy. Sean also advised me that Howard was complicated."

"Sean Riley?"

Was Sandy blushing? "Yeah. I ran into him..."

Sandy rose. "Looks like you have company."

I knew Russ stood at the boardwalk sliding glass door without looking. I swallowed hard. Reckoning time.

Sandy's self-preservation skills needed no fine-tuning. She waved to Russ and scooted out the opposite door with admirable haste. Not that I blamed her. I didn't want to be here facing Russ either. I considered retreat, but the sexy sweep of his dark hair framing his blue-fire gaze melted my resistance. Who could ignore those well-defined swimmer's shoulders carrying two Thai carryout bags from my favorite restaurant and a bottle of the green wine we'd discovered at a Portuguese wine tasting?

I waved him in, ready for anything except Bayle's sudden tirade. I covered my ears. How did he go from sound asleep to bark-mania so quickly? He'd even darted across my living room to the door in a blink.

"Bayle, quiet." He barked on undeterred, not even an iota of acknowledgement. So much for obedience. A single, no-nonsense, big-dog bark stopped him mid-tirade. Bayle plopped to the floor, commando style, as a lion-cut, brown-and-white-chested Portuguese Water Dog approached with purpose. Just above knee height, his fluffy white snout nudged my bulging treat pocket.

"Did I pass Matata's inspection?" Trust Russ to become an instant Barkviewian, chameleon-like, by borrowing his mother's dog.

"It'll cost you a treat to avoid anarchy." Russ kissed my cheek.

If that translated into two barking dogs, I'd give up the whole treat stash. I tossed both dogs heart-shaped cookies. Caught mid-air, both were wolfed down in a single gulp.

"What brand is that? Matata tends to be picky," Russ said.

"Rayelle's personal recipe. Want a taste?" I half-expected him to take a bite. He might have, but Matata intercepted the treat mid-toss and swallowed it whole.

"I do have a new respect for bribery." I pointed at the Thai food bags.

"When in doubt…" Russ moved right into my kitchen. He plated the food on Serengeti-inspired dinnerware and poured two glasses of wine into animal-stemmed glassware. "Sunset looks promising. Outside okay?"

I glanced toward the ocean. The sun sat low on the horizon, casting an inviting, golden glow over the Pacific. Not a low cloud in sight. "Are you sure?"

"It's a chamber of commerce moment," Russ insisted.

Arguably the busiest thoroughfare in Barkview, the sunset beach-walk provided everything but privacy. His choice. I grabbed two forks, tiger-striped napkins, and my sunglasses. The lead murder investigator cozying up to this reporter wasn't going to hurt my investigation any.

The dogs shadowed us to the patio and settled under the

table, Matata at Russ's feet and Bayle quivering against my leg. He relaxed more when I scratched his head.

I glanced up and down the boardwalk while Russ set the plates on the round teak table and pulled out the tan-striped, cushioned chair for me. His old-fashioned manners always made me feel special.

Russ raised his wine glass. "To…"

"Catching Howard's murderer." That just slipped out. Why did I always wreck the peace?

"And so we will." He took a long swallow, unfazed.

"Together?" The fresh, fizzy gooseberry essence washed over my tastebuds. The wine wasn't really Dr. Seuss green. Its name came from the Vinho Verde region in northern Portugal. The flavors complimented the spicy Thai food perfectly.

I smiled and waved to a gawking Gabby, who stumbled over Sal's coltish legs in failed nonchalance. Lead story on the morning news couldn't get word out of our intimate dinner any faster.

I bit back a smile at Russ's clenched jaw. He'd learn the Barkviewian your-business-is-everybody's-business creed soon enough.

I raised my glass. "Welcome to Barkview."

"You did try to warn me. For the record I will be taking your advice in the future."

I only nodded. I could be amiable too. "Let's enjoy the pad Thai. Smells like you ordered extra chili the way I like it."

Who could argue with noodles stir-fried in a rich sweet-savory fusion sauce with shrimp and dusted with crushed peanuts? Russ being in town would definitely affect my waistline.

We ate in compatible silence until Russ leaned back in his chair, his wine glass in hand. "Don't blink or you'll miss the green flash."

The globe dipped below the horizon. He sipped his wine. "Next time."

"More like when the time is right," I said.

"Have you seen it?"

I nodded. "Once, years ago. The sky was different that night."

"Are you familiar with the ancient Scottish myth that says if someone sees the green flash, they are incapable of being deceived in matters of sentiment and he who has been fortunate enough once to behold it is enabled to see closely into his own heart and to read the thoughts of others?"

And I'd thought it was just an atmospheric condition. "So, theoretically, I know your heart?"

Tingles followed his forefinger tracing my jawline. "I think you do."

I met his hot gaze for the first time.

"For the record, the chief did not offer the position freely," Russ said.

Bayle hopped to all fours in sync with my reaction. So there was more, much more to this after all. Was Howard Looc somehow involved in the investigation Russ had been working on in the area? No wonder Uncle G had protected him. "Is..."

Russ squelched my expectations. "I've already said too much. You know I can't share information about an ongoing investigation."

Or any other investigation, even when closed.

"But..." I bit my tongue. His crossed arms stopped me from going down that questioning avenue. "I know." I did know. The "keeping secrets" battle raged internally. It was my problem, not his. I had to get a grip if I expected this relationship to last. "Do you know who killed Howard?" I asked.

"No."

At least he hadn't shut me down entirely. "A knife in the back could indicate an act of passion," I suggested.

"Sometimes it does," Russ agreed.

"Howard never saw it coming. He still could've known his murderer. He just didn't feel threatened by them," I said. Russ's noncommittal hum irked me. "So, why is Rayelle a suspect?"

"Why shouldn't she be?" Russ countered.

Ugh. I thought Uncle G was a wall. Of course, Russ would be worse. "You know Rayelle. She catches and releases spiders."

"Her relationship with Howard is…"

"Unusual." His FBI profiler insight could help here.

I saw him struggle with what to say next and just sat back and waited for him to continue.

"Howard's Chinese upbringing is part of this equation."

"You mean he's more eastern in his strategies?" That made sense. Even Aunt Char admitted Howard was about the long game. Was that why he'd singled out Rayelle? Did he see her as the future of his flyball team?

Russ's attention turned to the rolling waves. He'd said all he was going to on the subject. "My aunt is Howard's executor. Is she in danger?"

"A detail has been assigned to her."

It was my turn to gape. "I don't understand. Uncle G said…"

"Cat." He took both of my hands in his warm ones. "We don't know anything yet. Trust me to do my job."

I did trust him. I squeezed his hands. "I can't just sit back and worry. I have to do something."

"I know. Follow the flyball angle."

It took a second for me to understand. He wanted my help on an angle he didn't perceive as dangerous to keep me busy. Not a bad strategy.

"And look for what?" I asked.

"A local connection to Howard's murder."

"Besides the Vespa Guardian?"

His eye roll summed up my opinion. Basking in his full attention, I nearly missed the implication. "A knife in the back doesn't fit your suspect's MO, does it?" No response, but based on his shrug, probably not. I could read him a little.

Options raced through my mind. Sean had the most to gain financially. Tina, Rayelle, and Howard formed a love triangle. As did Howard, Tina, and Stephan. Other barkery owners had a problem with Rayelle. The murder itself, inside Rayelle's shop with her own knife, potentially screamed personal. I patted my pocket for Post-its and a pen. Bayle nudged my foot as I felt a heart-shaped dog treat. What timing. I dropped the treat. He had been remarkably quiet. "You're not going to try to stop me from investigating?"

"Would it work?"

He knew me too well.

"Let me deal with the non-Barkview angle," he said. "Share when you have something."

A one-way share. More than I expected. "Do I need a fill-in for Rayelle's show?"

"Better to be prepared." He checked his fancy dive watch. "I am meeting Michelle Le Fleur at the Fluff and Buff tomorrow at eight a.m."

He had to know I planned to meet her as well. Meeting together indicated we were doing more than pursuing different angles. "Are you asking me to join you?"

"I am."

I set my elbows on the table, hoping that green flash legend was at least partly true. "Why?"

"From experience, I know she will talk freely to you."

I'd dropped that line to be included in the Cavalier investigation. "I'll meet you there."

"Make it at the alley at 7:45. Something is off in Michelle's statement."

Like Rayelle, Michelle lived in the apartment above her salon. Howard's car had been parked in the alley facing her bedroom window. "She isn't particularly detail-oriented."

"It's more than that."

I trusted his judgment. "Where are you staying?" With me would be awkward. With Uncle G might be a conflict.

"I have a room at the Old Barkview Inn until Wednesday. I rented a condo ten doors down." He pointed north.

My pulse jumped. A condo meant he planned to stay a while.

Matata rose with him. My hand brushed his as he picked up his plate. It clattered back down on the table. He wasn't immune to me. "You brought dinner. I'll clean up."

His eyes unwrinkled ever-so-slightly. "Deal. Same time tomorrow?"

I nodded. He cupped my face in both hands, his thumbs gently stroking my jaw. "I could get used to this."

So could I, I realized, watching him disappear down the boardwalk.

CHAPTER 12

My watch pinged the fifteen-minute reminder. I was going to be late meeting Russ. That weaponized pincushion loosely called a brush snagged in Bayle's hair yet again. He yelped and stutter-stepped backward, his hind legs slipping right off my granite bathroom counter. In retrospect, me, the ponytail queen, creating a powder-puff hairdo courtesy of YouTube couldn't possibly end well. Rayelle had called this grooming thing relaxing. I needed tranquilizers.

I dove with wide-receiver grace and caught Bayle before he hit the tile, both of us landing in a heap while my phone, two brushes, and a can of extra-stiff hairspray clanked end-over-end. We cringed in unison, neither of us breathing until peace reigned.

This was all Bayle's fault. If he hadn't tripped me with that brush right after breakfast, I'd never have noticed. After I took one look at his right-sided cotton-ball flop, his commando-crawl, paw-hiding-one-eye-retreat made perfect sense. No self-respecting Bichon could be seen in public without a proper buzz. The Cavalier queen, Renny, had taught me that some things were not negotiable. Clearly, I'd failed Bichon grooming. I'd even tried gathering his mane atop his head in a bow. That ended in a Rottweiler-fierce growl.

Ten minutes and counting until my scheduled meeting with Russ, time to make a decision. "First stop, the Fluff and Buff Salon." I stood, finally sure of my next move.

No way Bayle understood. Yet he scrambled across the tile to the garage door. Leash in his mouth, he stood with Easter-rabbit poise on his hind legs, with his front paws crossed, and waved. Yes, waved. The Bichon wave, Rayelle had called it. Who'd believe this? Too bad I couldn't get my phone out fast enough for a photo.

Who needed coffee after that?

I did, I realized two minutes after I'd turned onto First Street and stomped on the gas. Caffeine withdrawal hit me as I rummaged through my purse for my sunglasses. Bayle wasn't having any of it. Clipped to the seatbelt beside me, he huffed and nudged my wayward hand toward the steering wheel. No mistaking that move. Ugh! A passenger-seat driver, really? At least we were still only fashionably late.

"Okay. Okay." Forget the sunglasses. I adjusted my visor. It helped a little until the sun blinded me as I turned east onto Maple.

A glance down Third Street confirmed yellow tape still surrounded Bichon Bisquets. Uncle G's team had swarmed the place yesterday. What else could they possibly be processing?

I parked beside Russ's Land Rover on the alley corner adjacent to the Fluff and Buff. Of course, he was leaning against his car door, arms crossed. I swear Matata's posture mirrored his. Even though he was a borrowed dog, those two moved like one. Why did that dog-human link surprise me?

Russ opened my door as I struggled with Bayle's seatbelt. The aroma of caramel cappuccino wafted around me, teasing my taste buds and razor-sharpening my focus. Suddenly, the seatbelt released. Bayle tumbled across the leather seat. In one fluid move, I kissed Russ's cheek and snatched the Woofing Best cup.

"Good morning to you too," Russ said sardonically.

The tipped cup blocked the amusement I knew twinkled in his blue eyes. Not that I cared. I savored two long swallows, oblivious to everything but the warm liquid seeping through my body.

"Tough morning?" Russ asked.

"You'd never believe it." I handed him the coffee cup and lifted Bayle out of my SUV.

Russ's chuckle came out suspiciously like a croak. Bayle moaned and dive-bombed his head into my armpit, throwing me to the left. We would've both ended on the pavement if Russ hadn't steadied me.

"Guessing Bayle will be staying with Michelle." Russ motioned me to stand in the taped outline of Howard's parked car. A gabled rooftop peeked over the Hornbeam hedge. Only a high oval window, presumably in a bathroom, showed through the greenery. I pictured Michelle on tiptoes on her toilet seat, contorting every which way for a view. I glanced down the alley. Gem's Palace had a marginally better view from a back window. Howard had chosen the location carefully indeed. Only someone standing at the entrance to the alley could clearly see the car.

"Why would Michelle lie?" It made no sense.

"Don't know that she has yet. Her statement could merely be misleading," Russ suggested.

"She said she recognized the car. Unless she came outside..."

"Or she installed cameras since our last tour." Russ pointed to an oddly bulging branch in the greenery. The man had an eagle eye to pick that out of the branch chaos. "After the dognappings, she may have added security."

Michelle had been traumatized after Somerset had been dognapped while in her care.

"At the very least, I'd like to see her footage." Russ ushered me toward the front door, Matata falling in like a good sidekick. If only Bayle behaved as well. He tried to pull my arm out of the socket sniffing every pine cone.

At the glass door, Michelle whooshed out and air-kissed me, European-style. Dressed in a black smock with a gold logo over black pants and a cap-sleeve top, with a black beret dipped to the right on her poodle-puff hair, she embodied the famed Rive Gauche arts scene. A five-year resident of Barkview, Michelle's Champs-Élysées flair had elevated the canine coiffure scene to local acclaim.

One look at Bayle and Michelle's shriek sent every field mouse for miles to cover. "*Mon petit.* What have you done?" In a single move, she scooped Bayle into her arms and marched inside, her jet-black standard poodle, Fifi, in perfect step. "*Vien.* We will fix this. *Oui.*" Michelle's forefinger beckoned. Bayle just beamed, his long eyelashes fluttering with debutante innocence.

Ugh! Bichon grooming class here I come. At least I wasn't alone. Russ and Matata dutifully followed.

The Fluff and Buff's opulent Louis XV–style entry always notched up my Wright Dog Insanity, WDI, rating scale and sent me into sensory overload. Black and white harlequin painted pumpkins stacked in tree-shaped mounds decorated with Venetian-style masks just added more pressure. Only in Barkview could a dog-grooming parlor replicate the lavishness of the Grand Palais du Versailles.

I admired Russ and Matata's nonchalance as Michelle ushered us through the rococo waiting area, decorated with fancy Carnival masks I swear observed my every move, and into the main salon. Set up with individual stations in stunning baroque splendor, gilt mirrors fronted ornate tables with black-and-gold-rimmed sinks. We passed two groomers fussing over other dogs, finally stopping at a queenly, gold-edged table adjacent to the Entrée du Sanctuaire archway. Beyond those double doors a stately seven-foot hornbeam hedge protected a slate-colored sunporch where plush blue-and-white-striped cushions surrounded a babbling fountain.

"Kill me if I ever get this kind of décor," I whispered for Russ's ears only. Silence reigned, but I recognized the ever-so-slight brow arch as agreement. Matata remained in step until Michelle offered him a treat. Not any old treat, but one of her famous chamomile biscuits—the same treat Sandy used daily to subdue her overactive Jack Russell. The biscuits worked. Although still hyper by my standards, Jack's "terrorist" days had ended.

That biscuit was just right for *Fido's Food Fest*. I glanced at Michelle fretting over Bayle. Drama queens rarely played well on TV. My stomach clenched. Choosing someone other than a Barkview barkery owner would be a good solution to my hosting problem.

Never a good fence-sitter, I blurted out my thoughts. "Michelle, how would you like to share your chamomile biscuit recipe on *Fido's Food Fest* on Sunday? You can even pitch your shop and give a few grooming tips." Talk about a shot in the arm for her business. She couldn't buy that kind of publicity.

I expected a charming blush, not deer-in-the-headlights terror. "Go on *national* TV? *Absolument pas.*" No explanation. No chance to convince her to try. She just turned away, giving me a clear view of her smock ties.

Russ cut off my "But why?" Michelle had done well when

interviewed on *The Bark View* morning show. There was more to this than stage fright.

More confused than ever, I relinquished the lead to Russ. I patted my pockets. Post-its found. Naturally, no pen. Russ handed me his before I could ask. Was I really that predictable?

Fancy computer notebook and stylus pen ready, Russ asked, "The chief tells me you reported Bolt barking."

"Oui." Michelle set Bayle in the sink and wet his hair. From a fluff puff to drowned rat in fifty seconds. It was shocking how small and pink-skinned Bayle was beneath all that fuzz. "At 11:35 Fifi woke me up. I remember exactly because I looked at my clock. Fifi is a very light sleeper." Michelle air-kissed Fifi, sprawled at her side. "Every noise she wakes up for me to investigate."

"How did you investigate Bolt Looc's barking?" I had to admire Russ's casual tone.

"I looked and saw Bolt *frénétique* at the passenger window," Michelle responded easily. No hesitation.

"What room were you in?" Russ asked.

"My bedroom."

Russ's sidelong glance offered me the bad-cop role. "Michelle, you can't see the alley from your bedroom window."

She didn't miss a beat. "*Naturellement*. I checked my phone." Michelle wrapped Bayle in a fluffy towel and placed him on the grooming table. Bayle lounged on his side, eating up all the attention.

"Your phone?" Russ had been right again.

Michelle dried her hands, removed her phone from a smock pocket, and handed it to me. "The blue telescope icon. Press it. You can see the alley and the front door. No more dogs will be dognapped on my watch. The security system makes me feel safer." Her hand rested dramatically in the vicinity of her heart.

Russ had called that one, too. The icon wasn't exactly a telescope; it looked more like an antique spyglass. Hmm. It was the same company Rayelle had purchased her security system from. Coincidence? Maybe. A pursuable lead for sure.

"Does Rayelle know about your cameras?" I asked.

"I don't know. I suggested she get a camera after the pranksters continued to bother her. I never told her I had one."

"How did you find the camera company?" Research and execution didn't really fit Michelle.

"Alan Thorpe suggested the company. Uses them to watch his Golden. It's a doggie cam, too."

Another link to Alan. I needed to see him this afternoon.

"Did you tell Officer Richardson about the cameras?" Russ asked.

Michelle scratched her chin. "I told him what I saw. I don't remember if the cameras came up."

Her forced nonchalance failed. Russ and I shared a look. It wasn't the first time I'd thought Michelle wasn't being entirely truthful. But what could she be hiding?

Since I had some familiarity with the camera's fuzzy imagery, I had to ask, "How did you know it was Howard's car?" The shape and color were likely clear enough, but Howard didn't have a monopoly on black Mercedes in Barkview.

"Mr. Looc parked there all the time."

"How often is all the time?" Russ inquired.

"Mostly on Tuesdays, after Barklay Park flyball practice."

"So, he's been there every Tuesday night for the last month?" I wanted to believe Rayelle, but...

"Since I set up the cameras in August."

The visits had started before Rayelle moved to Barkview? Canines on Canvas Gallery had been the previous tenants. The husband-and-wife team had displayed dog-centric artists and sculptures for a little less than a year before family issues had caused them to move back to Ohio. Leaving Barkview to return to the Midwest seemed suspect, but that was another story. Why would Howard have visited them so often? Or had he? A landlord key allowed him building access anytime he wanted. But why would Howard need a clandestine meeting place?

"What camera views do you have?" Russ asked.

"Alley entry area, front door, and Sanctuaire."

"I'd like all angles from Sunday night." Russ made a note.

"*Bien sûr*. I heard a strange noise right after Bolt started barking."

"What kind of noise?" I asked.

Michelle threw her hands up. "I think it was the Vespa Guardian."

"Why?" Russ seemed to lose patience.

"I heard a *rat-ta-ta. Rat-ta-ta. Voorum. Rat-ta-ta. Gunshot. Voorum.*" Michelle closed her eyes, remembering.

"Like a car backfiring?" I asked.

"*Non. Everyday* Stephan's car back-fires when he enters the roundabout. This sound was different."

I scribbled more notes and stuffed them in my bulging pocket. If a Vespa really was in the area, it could explain how the murderer escaped.

"A scooter?" I suggested. Better to eliminate options at this stage.

She shook her head. "*Non.*"

Russ tapped his stylus pen on the screen until he located the Vespa video. "Is this what you heard?"

"*Oui. Exactement.* I told you it was the Vespa Guardian."

If she was so sure, why did she sound surprised?

"Now, we fix Bayle. *Attention.*" The same scary brushes I'd tortured Bayle with lay within Michelle's reach. She chose the pin brush first. "You start with short, smooth strokes to detangle." His eyes half closed, Bayle lay on his side, loving every minute. "Think of how you brush your own hair. One hundred strokes a night..."

Seriously? Who did that? I nodded anyway.

Bayle turned over at Michelle's command. She brushed quickly before exchanging the pin brush for a small-toothed comb. "Now, you comb out the debris." She handed it to me. "You try on his tail."

Ugh! Who knew what those dark specks stuck in his white hair were. First stroke and the comb caught. I pulled harder. Bayle yelped. The comb clattered on the table.

"*Patience.* Do you like having your hair pulled?" Michelle asked. "Here, work the knot out with your fingers." Michelle combed out a piece of bark, a shell, and artificial grass blades, among other things, from Bayle's tail.

I exhaled, begging for divine intervention. Russ's straight face failed to hide the amused twinkle in his eyes. Even Matata toyed with me. Being mocked by a dog had to be an all-time low. My finger jammed on something hard. A small pebble, maybe. Rayelle had warned me Bayle's hair was like a Swiffer duster. This thing had been cocooned in white hair. I tugged and pulled until the debris fell in my hand. The pebble was not smooth at all, but faceted on one side. The stone slipped out of my fingers as I held it to the light. Michelle retrieved it and held it under the water.

Water beaded on the stone. "Ah. Coated in oil." She dunked a toothbrush in sudsy water and scrubbed. Satisfied, she held the eighth-of-an-inch sphere up to the light.

I was no diamond expert by any means, but I did have an affinity for all things that glittered. Living close to the Gemology Institute of America (GIA) main campus, I had indulged in too many classes on gemstone identification not to recognize this one. The color was decent. Cut poor. Clarity okay. Fire almost nonexistent. All characteristics of an old European-cut antique diamond. The kind found in estate jewelry deemed too valuable to sell but too ugly to wear. The stone must've fallen out of an old setting. Where in the world could Bayle have picked that up?

The dog had been at the crime scene, but since his last grooming, he'd also been on countless outdoor walks, to Petronics, KDOG, the police station and Ciao Bella Dolce... Don't ask me how I knew, but it had something to do with Howard's murder. Although I couldn't legally isolate the diamond's origin, it could eliminate suspects. Tina, for example, wore a five-carat solitaire. My aunt owned the most recognizable old world diamonds in town. If one of the stones was missing from the antique Cavalier-shaped pins only taken out for exhibition, I refused to contemplate the ramifications.

If someone needed to replace a diamond, Ariana Papas, the co-owner of Gem's Palace, would know about it.

"That is quite a treasure," Michelle announced. "These are my finds." She lifted the lid on a silver box on her table, displaying earth-toned stones and shell fragments.

Russ pocketed the diamond as I continued combing Bayle until his hair crackled and my fingers ached. All the while, Bayle lounged like a sunbather with nothing but time.

Michelle nodded her approval. "Now, we style." She picked up the blow dryer and the pin brush. "You brush upward. Toward the face. Like a lion's mane."

On a dog? Talk about counterintuitive. This was insane. I didn't preen like this for black-tie events. No way I'd fuss over a dog. "How about I bring Bayle in for a brush every morning?"

Michelle saw dollar signs. "Bien sur. *Mais.* You can cut his hair shorter. It is easier to manage."

And have Rayelle murder me? No, thank you. If she was willing to give up valuable time to primp and spoil Bayle, who was I to say otherwise? "How about an 8 a.m. standing appointment?"

Bayle agreed with a tail wag. Great. I could be rid of him for a few hours a day. A win-win.

Michelle completed Bayle's grooming while Russ downloaded her surveillance recordings.

Drawn to the fresh scent of his sandalwood cologne, I leaned over his shoulder. I could stay here all day. "Anything helpful?" I'd experienced enough dog primping to last a lifetime. Talk about personal motivation to find the metallic blob garment from Rayelle's video.

"I don't know. I'll send you a copy."

"After you send it to the lab to be cleaned up."

Russ nodded. "Maybe they can isolate the noise Michelle heard. All I hear is Bolt's barking."

"Spoken like a non–dog owner. Michelle can tune out barking like no one I've ever met."

"A helpful ability in Barkview." He yawned.

"Didn't sleep well?" I'd been thinking about him last night, too.

"Matata snores."

"So does Bayle. Earplugs work."

Russ closed the flap on his notebook and checked his watch. "I have thirty minutes to accompany you to Gem's Palace. Ariana may have some insight into this diamond."

He'd read my mind. I still hesitated. "You want to go to a jewelry store with me?"

"Is that a problem?" His gaze probed mine for answers.

"No. I rarely get out of there without a bauble or three." There. I admitted it.

Russ chuckled. "Never figured you for an easy sell."

With jewelry... "Ariana's a pro."

"I've met Ariana," he reminded me.

"Not on her turf."

"I can hold my own."

No doubt, but... Never mind. Like dinner on the boardwalk, he'd figure it out. "Don't say I didn't warn you."

"Noted." Matata moved in step with Russ.

Bayle looked like his normal poofy self again. He bounced to my side, tossing his head, seemingly fascinated with his hair ripple until I scratched him. I laughed. I couldn't help myself. He did have childlike exuberance covered.

I paid for Bayle's makeover and followed Russ toward the two-story, emerald-trimmed Victorian framed by endless magenta bougainvillea and fall foliage accents. Although Ariana and Chris had not reported Bolt's barking or anything unusual, we still needed to ask. Maybe they popped Ambien nightly. A high-end jewelry store seemed a likely candidate for additional security. Maybe they also had cameras.

I remained optimistic until we turned the corner onto Third Street.

"So, that's the famous Aphrodite's Haven," Russ remarked.

Morning sunlight glistened off the porch swing framed by potted blush roses and fall pumpkins.

"You know about that?" My cheeks warmed.

"Everyone who is anyone in Barkview knows that proposing on that swing portends a blissful marriage," Russ remarked.

"So Ariana says." I couldn't meet his not-so-innocent gaze.

"A skeptic?"

I shrugged. What did I know about romance anyway? "I like the sentiment."

"Careful, someone might realize you are a romantic at heart."

I expected a mocking grin, not curiosity. "I'm as much a happily-ever-after fan as the next girl."

"Good." His boyish smile held promise, the heart-skipping kind, as he held the leaded glass door open into fantasyland. No doubt the mirrored ceiling helped, but I swear glittering prisms dipped and swayed before my eyes like dancers in *Swan Lake*. The aroma of sugarplums wrapped around me. Seven octagonal glass counters housed whimsical creations by world-class goldsmith Christos Papas. Flanked by three buttery leather armchairs, the mini-islands invited delightful gawking. I sank into an armchair. Russ sat beside me, Matata at his feet. Bayle squeezed between my legs and the chair, pressing against one leg.

Too much? Maybe for some. To me it felt like a warm hug. From dangling pendants and pins to bracelets, studded collars, and dog tags, canines of all kinds twinkled in artful Victorian clutter. Scary Halloween skull pendants in sterling caught my eye.

"Good morning." Ariana's pleasure mirrored Gem's, the tan-and-black German Shepherd at her side. "Welcome. It is good to have you back in Barkview, Russ." A trace of her European heritage sounded in her vowels. Barely five feet, two inches tall in heels, Ariana's lithe form made her polo shirt, slacks, and coordinating plaid sweater looped around her neck look both fashionable and timeless.

"Good morning, Ariana." Russ introduced Matata.

Ariana coaxed the dog to her side with a treat. "He's a sweet boy."

Matata gobbled the snack before trotting back to Russ. "He's my mother's dog."

No surprise in Ariana's grin. "A Portuguese Water Dog is a good choice for allergy sufferers. So is a Bichon."

I hadn't really thought about it, but Russ hadn't sneezed anywhere near as much as when my aunt's Cavalier had been in residence.

Bayle interrupted further comment by wiggling through my legs and barking—the throw-the-ball-already bark I dreaded. I swear Matata rolled his eyes. I patted my pockets helplessly.

Like magic, Ariana pulled a ball out of nowhere and rolled it across the wood floor. "Here, Bayle." In a puff of white, Bayle darted after it.

"We're here for your help." No need to play coy. Let the ritual begin.

"I see." She assessed my wandering eye. "I have a gift for you."

"A gift?" I sat up straight. No hard sell? Talk about disarmed-on-arrival. "Are you feeling okay?"

"You tell me." Ariana removed a slim velvet bracelet box from behind the counter. "For you, Cat, to remember your journey."

"A journey? I'm not going anywhere." Except maybe to producer's hell if I didn't find a suitable chef to fill in for Rayelle.

More than a little distracted, I tossed the ball Bayle dropped on my feet. The ball ricocheted off the glass case and arced upward, an ornate, seven-years-bad-luck mirror in its path. Time slowed to a crawl as the ball swished through a collar display, tapped the mirror, and thankfully bounced on the floor.

Crisis averted, Ariana beamed. "Life is a journey. Open it."

A deeper meaning? Not now. I lifted the lid. On black velvet sat a delicate bracelet, its peanut-links resembling dog bones with two charms attached. I recognized the Cavalier with the slim diamond collar right away. The second was a powder-puff Bichon. "I don't understand." But I did, all too well.

"A charm bracelet represents memories. Some good, some maybe not," Ariana said.

"Thank you. I think." Good and bad had come out of my time with Renny. Bayle ended that trip down memory lane, dropping the ball at my feet and wiggling puppy-like. Lesson learned. I rolled the ball this time.

"You try until you find the right fit." Ariana stroked Gem's ears.

"I'm only watching Bayle." Rayelle had better claim him before I lost my mind.

"Posh. Nothing wrong with taking a test drive. Better to know what you're getting into."

Now that was a vision. "I'm not a…"

I swear Matata, Bayle, and Gem stared right at me. Except for a raised brow, Russ remained maddeningly neutral.

"Not a what, exactly?" Ariana inquired. I'd asked for that pointed question. "Honestly, you never know until you live with them."

Visions of Russ in boxers in my kitchen filled my thoughts. He cleared his throat, clearly reading my mind. "You're killing me, Cat."

I almost refocused until his fingers lingered on my wrist as he clasped the chain. The gold bracelet twinkling in the fluorescent lights finally did it. A journey. Ariana had no idea, right?

I placed the antique diamond on the counter. No need to say a thing.

Ariana considered then louped the stone. "Old European cut. Art Deco era. The stone is worn. Look." She handed me the jeweler's magnifier. "See the nicks on the table. Fifty-six facets. Hand cut. Symmetry is adequate. If I were to guess, I'd say it's from an eternity band. Quality is fair. Not Celeste Barklay's."

I breathed easier. No Aunt Char connection.

"Where did you find this?" Ariana asked.

Bayle swung his tail and barked his "Who, me?" bark. Russ and I shared a glance. No way he'd understood. Or did he?

"Ah. Good Swiffer." Ariana tossed the ball. Bayle merely jogged after it this time. He really was tiring out. "Bichons' tails bring in all kinds of things. I had a client who lost her wedding ring. Looked everywhere. Finally found it two days later... never mind."

My gaze strayed to my bare left hand. Proof positive jewelry stores were off limits with boyfriends. "Anyone looking for an antique diamond?"

"The younger generation wants sparkle and fire," Ariana said.

Yeah. Round brilliants worked for me, too. I ignored Russ's look. Well, tried to. I felt my cheeks heat anyway.

"I will ask around."

Russ smiled. "Thank you. I need to ask you about the night Howard Looc was killed."

Ariana shared an oversized chair with Gem, who huddled beside her. "Chris and I are early risers. We go to bed by ten. Gem barked a little after midnight."

"Do you know what woke her?" I eyed the Shepherd. If only she could talk.

Ariana shook her head. "I thought I heard a gunshot."

Russ referred to his tablet. "You didn't mention that to the police."

"No. Chris thought it sounded like Stephan's car backfiring."

A tad different from Michelle's story. I made a note. "You disagree?"

"Yes. Stephan's car chokes, and then backfires. This was more like a gunshot."

She sounded sure. How could Ariana possibly be an authority?

"Does Stephan drive by often?" Russ asked.

"Only on surf's up nights. He sleeps in his car to get first break."

Her accented surf lingo took me a minute to understand. "You follow the surf reports?" That seemed odd.

"Heavens no. I play darts at the Royal Bull."

No doubt well from the way she checked out her manicure. Russ made a note.

"Stephan occasionally comes in after his G&G tour ends," Ariana added.

"Did Stephan play Sunday night?" Russ asked.

"No. He arrived, but Stephanie called before he ordered his drink. He said someone no-showed and she needed his help at the yogurt shop."

That corroborated the twin's story.

"Did you hear any other vehicle noises?" I asked.

Ariana shook her head.

"The police report says you did not see Howard's car in the alley until the police arrived," Russ said.

"Correct."

Odd that neither she nor Chris had looked out their bedroom window. If I'd heard what I thought might be a gunshot, I'd be on the floor with my head down while Russ would be running to the rescue. Would Chris dive for cover or be a hero? Zero curiosity didn't seem exactly right either.

"Have you seen Howard's car parked in the alley before?" I asked.

Ariana shook her head.

I noted motion sensors and red lights blinking on the walls. "What security system do you use?"

"The building was a bank before we purchased it. It already had a complex alarm system."

For 1980-something. "Have you added video?" I asked.

"Upstairs." Ariana rushed to explain. "A doggie cam for Gem."

To watch a dog versus their expensive merchandise? Said something about what Ariana valued. "Why haven't you upgraded to video surveillance in the shop?"

"Barkview is very safe, but times change. We've been considering a plan from Trooper TC Security. They call me weekly."

Another link to Trooper TC Security. I added them to my need-to-contact list. Would the clues ever make sense?

CHAPTER 13

Russ and I parted at our vehicles. He headed to the police station while I drove to Petronics to meet with Alan Thorpe. I envisioned Howard's sardonic grin as I passed J. Tracker's glaring corporate presence enroute.

Today a handful of cars filled Petronics' parking lot. No trouble locating Alan's white Escalade. The 'Just Throw It' Golden Retriever flyball decal gave it away.

Like many Barkview business leaders, Alan Thorpe and I attended many of the same charity events. Other than exchanging greetings, we'd never really talked, necessitating Aunt Char to arrange the meeting.

After clearing security, Alan met me inside. The man's dancing brown eyes framed by bushy blond brows and shiny bald head reminded me of a happy Buddha in a MMA wrestler's body. His Golden Retriever, Hawn, stood serenely at his side. At least, she appeared tranquil. I sensed a pent-up energy in them both bubbling just beneath the surface.

Alan politely shook my hand, reserving a truly warm greeting for Bayle. He scratched the dog's head and threw a red tennis ball with major league precision down the flyball-framed hallway. Like a runner in the blocks, Hawn sprinted into action. Not to be beaten, Bayle darted after the larger dog, quickly making up ground, his smaller legs somehow matching pace until the ball bounced off the wall. Midair Bayle snagged the ball, spun and started back strides ahead of the Golden Retriever.

Alan's jaw-dropping awe said it all. "Whoa. Howard was dead on about Bayle."

His words and the faint smell of rich cigars clinging to his golf shirt distracted me for a second. "You doubted him?"

Alan shook his head. "Seeing is still believing. Practice is tomorrow at 6 p.m. sharp. Don't be late. I'm a dog short. Possibly two if Bolt isn't up to speed."

I must've gaped at him. His boss had just been murdered and Alan worried about a flyball practice? Was this pure fanaticism or something more?

Alan spoke quickly. "I mean no disrespect. Howard planned for this moment for years. My honor demands I execute his vision."

I believed him, I realized. Apparently, Howard didn't have exclusivity on manipulation. If I refused, would this meeting end differently?

"Sure." Rayelle had better be free by then.

"Howard was a true visionary and friend." He caught Bayle before the dog skidded into the wall. Hawn backpedaled to a stop at my feet. What Alan lacked in hospitality, his Golden Retriever made up for in tail-shaking excitement and a nose-dive to my private parts.

I leaped back. Hawn kept coming. "Hey. Hey."

"She's just shaking hands." Alan's smile softened his frown.

"Can she do it from over there?"

"Hawn. Down." The retriever lay down at my feet, panting.

If only Bayle listened that well. "I, uh, know you are busy. Thank you for seeing me." Not that he would've missed an opportunity to meet Bayle.

"You have no idea. Petronics is a family business."

I understood all too well after Aunt Char's past illness. "How long have you worked with Howard?"

Alan tossed the ball again. Both dogs bolted as he ushered me toward his office.

"Five years. Howard hired me as a project manager at J. Tracker." We entered a utilitarian office overlooking the same Zen garden Howard's office fronted. Hawn went straight through the doggie door to the grass. Bayle head-bumped the Retriever-accommodating door flap twice before getting enough momentum to scurry through.

Alan motioned for me to sit on the leather sofa. Like Howard's office, an immaculate, smoked-glass L-shaped desktop held a computer docking station, a screen, and a calculator. I focused on the two framed photographs behind the desk. One pictured a blonde woman dressed for motocross; the other, a Golden Retriever.

"Is that Hawn?"

"It's Hawn's father, Goldie. He was flyball royalty."

No missing his reverence. Or the link. "Is that how you met Howard?"

"Yes. My team, the Golden Rule, eliminated Howard's rival in the semifinals at the national qualifier five years ago in June. He made me an offer to run his team before the finals."

"Howard won the championship." No need to ask. I knew the answer.

Alan nodded. "The man understood strategy. I learned more from playing chess with him than all my advanced degrees."

Howard rewarded talent well. "You were bribed."

Alan's chuckle made no sense. "I was given a chance to build a dynasty."

"You already had a winning team."

"I had a declining team. Howard recognized Goldie's illness. He advised me to breed him quickly. I'm glad I listened. Goldie died from inoperable cancer six months after Hawn's birth."

"So, you came to work for Howard."

"I agreed to manage his flyball team. I started working for Howard six months later when he told me about his implantable medical tracker invention. I wanted in. Goldie may have had a chance if I'd treated his cancer earlier."

Another passionate believer. Howard certainly knew how to motivate people. "Did you fire Tina's dog from the flyball team?"

Alan would not meet my gaze. "I did."

"At Howard's urging?"

He hesitated. "Not exactly. Bella isn't well. Tina is in denial."

Interesting. The dog did look lethargic. "How did you know?"

"Same symptoms as Goldie. I told her to see a vet."

"Did she?"

"The vet cleared Bella, but there's something wrong. I saw three vets before Goldie's diagnosis. Tina accused me of being a worry-wart. She refused to seek another opinion."

"Yet you were sure?"

He nodded. "So was Howard. Adamant, in fact. Said he knew the dog."

What was I missing? How could Howard have been that sure when medical science found nothing? I thought about the experimental injectable. Could he have injected Bella with the device? Was that ethical?

"So you made the hard choice?" I asked.

Alan nodded. "Howard supported my call. He told me he'd recruited Bayle afterward."

Was it really about Bella? Howard wasn't above a little manipulation. No sense arguing with a true believer. "At the cost of his marriage? He had to know what Tina would do."

"That woman is Vesuvius. I admit I never expected her to run right to Sean." Alan spat Howard's nemesis's name.

"How did Howard react?"

"He laughed. Mumbled something about destiny. I couldn't believe it. Tina was his light; Bianca and Joey his air."

"Yet he left them."

"So it seems." Another insider questioning Howard's motives?

"Do you think he planned to go back to Tina?"

Alan stretched his neck. "I think Howard would do anything to keep Tina and the kids safe."

His insight got me thinking. Could I forgive Russ for doing whatever it took to protect me? Emotion pooled in my stomach just thinking about being loved like that.

"Why did Tina need to be safe?" Learning why seemed to be the crux of everything.

"I don't know. Howard hadn't been himself for the last six months. He moved to the casino. Canceled our chess games and isolated himself."

I believed him. It all suddenly made sense. Something had happened—something that involved the FBI. Had Howard been working with Russ when I'd met him? No wonder he'd been available when the Cavaliers had been dognapped.

"What changed?" Someone had to know.

Alan ran his hand over his head. "I wish I knew. Jen noticed it too."

"Who's Jen?"

"Jen Russo owns Roxie." Alan pointed to a flyball photo on the shelf beside him. "The fourth dog on our team."

I should've known. "I don't know her."

"The chief vouched for her."

My intuition twinged. "She worked with Uncle G in the military?" Where else would he know her from?

Alan nodded. "Roxie was a lucky find."

Or part of a bigger plan. "What does Jen do?"

"She's a dog handler at Trooper TC. She came to town to be a part of our team."

Another recruit. Sandy needed to look into her. "So what changed with Howard?"

Alan's head shake said it all. "I don't know. I've analyzed everything. Six months ago, the status quo just changed."

Which clearly made Alan crazy. "Was there a technology breakthrough?" The J. Tracker documents I'd discovered predated this timeline.

"Not that I'm aware of."

As the general manager he'd know. "Can I talk to F. Hazing?"

"Who?" Alan's confusion seemed genuine.

"He worked with Howard on the injectable project."

"Don't know him. Spell the name for me."

Alan scribbled the letters on a pad. "Howard liked word games, anagrams in particular. He especially liked melding his Chinese heritage with American culture. His original flyball team name was Foxing Each Pi. I changed it to Outfoxing Pi. Easier for everyone to remember."

"Howard didn't mind?"

"Took me a while to convince him. I kept his fascination with the number pi."

As if that explained it. The anagram interest did open a new area for investigation, though. "Did you win when you played chess with Howard?"

"Twice. The night Howard hired me and once last month. His head was someplace else. He kept talking about his legacy."

"At forty?" Could Howard's Chinese heritage be at play here?

"I know. Legacy generally comes in your late fifties when you start thinking about retirement. During that last game he also said something odd."

I leaned in. This seemed important. "What was that?"

"My children need to know I have done the right thing."

Which was what, exactly?

CHAPTER 14

"In addition to digging up information on Jen Russo, you want me to figure out the meaning of a possible eight-letter Chinese anagram?" Sandy's you-can't-be-serious glare did trigger doubt.

Being crammed into the phone booth we called a studio control room two hours before preproduction start-up for my aunt's show *Throw Him a Bone* didn't help my case any.

"Something major changed in Howard's life six months ago. F. Hazing is the best clue I have." The only real clue except for the Vespa ghost.

"You do know there are like forty thousand options and I don't speak Chinese either, right? Do you even know what dialect Howard spoke?"

Doubts mounted. "He came from southern China. Isn't that Cantonese?"

Sandy tapped the keys on her computer. "Or Hakka. Or, knowing Howard, ancient Mandarin. Why are you asking me? Russ has resources. I thought you two were working together."

I hated to admit it, but... "Define together."

"I see." She did, much to my annoyance. "And you need to prove you can figure this out on your own?"

Childish? Guilty. "There has to be a way." Sandy's crossed arms stated her opinion. "I'm hoping Joey can help. Alan tells me Howard played word games with his son."

"Your backup plan is to rely on a nine-year-old American's grasp of Chinese?"

Verbalized it sounded crazy. My fingers caught in my tangled bangs. This drive to uncover secrets had to stop. "I'm losing my mind."

Sandy patted my arm. "You know this is a long shot. Let me be clear. A moon shot." At least she hadn't completely shut me down. "Do you have anything else to narrow the search?"

I shared Alan's insight into Foxing Each Pi/Outfoxing Pi. "Whatever this big secret is, it's overshadowing the investigation."

"Or are you just letting it?"

I exhaled. I really hated it when she went psychologist on me.

Sandy relented. "On another note, has Rayelle been charged?"

"Not yet. The sixty-hour clock is still ticking."

"That's something."

"Not much. Michelle insists she heard the Vespa Guardian. Ariana heard a backfire or gunshot. She doesn't think it was Stephan's Bug. Rayelle remains the only plausible suspect."

"We've all heard Stephan's Beetle backfiring."

"Problem is that his car sounds like a high-speed sewing machine. Nothing like the noise Michelle described. Why would he drive a distinctive car three blocks, anyway? Wouldn't he just walk?"

Sandy chewed her lip. "Sorry I asked. Have you found a guest chef to fill in for Rayelle?"

"Not yet. Mel is my last choice."

"Planning on cable suicide?"

Probably. "I'm running out of options. We can use the Sunday taping for Wednesday as planned, but I don't have backup episodes. The show is too new to rerun an episode. I'm open to ideas for a fill-in segment."

"The ratings will take a hit."

No kidding. My world lived and died on ratings. I needed a miracle.

"How are you and Bayle getting along?" Sandy asked.

Snoring, with a paw laid across my foot like a fluffy sandal strap, he looked cute and cuddly. "He's, uh, a handful." To say the least.

"Russ isn't allergic to him."

"Ariana pointed that out, too."

"In front of the engagement ring counter, no doubt."

"Nothing shocks Russ." I really liked that about him.

"Maybe he just hides it well," Sandy said.

Something to think about. "What's the big deal about allergies? The pills work."

"It's a lot to ask someone to live on pills to breathe for the rest of their life."

"I hadn't really thought about it that way."

"Maybe you should."

But I didn't want to think about Russ's loyalty or how he made me feel. I wanted to be mad about the secrets he kept.

Sandy should be gloating, not chewing her lip. "What are you afraid to tell me?" I asked.

"Sean invited me and Jack to dinner Wednesday after the show."

"Sean Riley?" Was J. Tracker's owner looking for inside information? If he hurt Sandy...

"I know you don't like him."

"I don't trust him." An understatement, really. Too many unanswered questions involving Howard and questionable business practices existed. "Are you considering it?"

"He invited my dog, too."

No secret the direct path to Sandy's heart involved her dog. I flopped into the nearest chair. Sandy's last boyfriend had been part of a conspiracy to kill me. How could she even consider dating another man with dubious motives? "And that makes everything okay?"

Sandy inspected her manicure. "No. It doesn't. I want to say Sean's not involved, but considering my history I can't be sure."

I squeezed Sandy's arm. "Hey. We were both fooled."

Sandy exhaled. "It's making me question everything. I'll see what I can come up on your anagram. I have to know someone who speaks Cantonese."

No doubt Sandy would locate a Chinese linguist passionate about letter scrambling. Talking to Joey couldn't hurt.

I detoured to the Sit and Stay Café for a family-sized mac and cheese casserole on my way to Tina Looc's. I remembered the emotional roller-coaster right after my uncle passed too well. Every thoughtful meal delivered really was one less detail to worry about.

I headed south on Fifth Street and drove past the police station. "I'm not checking up on Russ. It's on the way to the Terraces," I remarked to no one.

Bayle wasn't buying any of it. Front paws crossed on my passenger seat, his head cocked to the right, he just blinked those enviable peachy-white lashes at me.

I huffed. "Okay. Maybe I am spying." Seeing his Land Rover still reassured me. I continued to the Terraces turnoff and zigzagged up the eucalyptus-lined road.

Located south of downtown with a peekaboo view of the

rugged coastline, the Loocs' restored mansard-roofed home had an almost gothic elegance. Set behind intricately curved iron gates, the expansive lawn doubled as a soccer or flyball field. Halloween witches meandered among gravestones leading to the porch.

I parked behind Tina's Mercedes in the circular drive. Silver-panned casserole in one hand, I attempted to free Bayle with the other. The seatbelt released on the third attempt, vanquishing visions of splattered cheese on the pavers. Accolades for my dog-handling skills died the second the front door opened and a black-and-white blur lunged at me. Instinct took over. I backed up two steps. Bayle dove right between my legs, barking like a lunatic. Omg! Half the size of a Border Collie, Bayle didn't stand a chance!

Ready to defend, I leaped forward. Except Bayle didn't need my help. Tail fanning and nose to privates, the dogs sniffed each other. These two dogs knew each other well.

Tina caught the casserole pan as it slipped from my fingers. "Bolt. Down." The dog obeyed.

My turn. "Bayle. Down." I mimicked her command and tone exactly. No luck. Like a white tornado, Bayle dashed to Bolt, barking.

"Bayle. Down." Tina's voice stopped him cold. With disobedience no longer an option, Bayle's belly hit the floor.

Stunned, I just stared.

"That dog needs to know who's the alpha."

Clearly, not me. My past lack of tolerance for misbehaving dogs seemed hypocritical right now.

Tina motioned to Nonna, hovering inside the doorway.

"*Buon pomeriggio*, Catalina." Dressed in a stark black housedress, Nonna relieved Tina of the dish. She scurried inside, her steps surprisingly catlike. Not that I'd ever admit that out loud.

"Grazie." Tina's somber black dress with a white lace hankie spilling from her sleeve did not hide her nervous energy. "Come in."

I followed Tina into the black-and-white marble hallway. Guarded by two lions, dramatic best described the expansive staircase in the two-story entry. We entered a side parlor. This shrine to flyball greatness overwhelmed while explaining so much. A lifetime of framed photos and painstakingly polished trophies lined the walls under the watchful stare of the Looc family portrait mounted above the fireplace.

"Howard loved this room," Tina sniffled. "I-I don't want to leave it."

The room remained unchanged, even though Howard had moved out six months ago. "I'm so sorry, Tina."

Tina dabbed her red-rimmed eyes. "So am I."

I empathized with her glare at Bayle. Sexual or not, something had been going on between Rayelle and Howard. Being Rayelle's friend and advocate put me in the line of fire. I braced myself.

"Thank you for getting Bolt released to me." Tina motioned for me to sit on the leather sofa.

"He's part of your family." Deep down, Tina knew that, too.

"I wondered."

"Wondered what?"

"If Alan would get custody of Bolt."

"Alan?" I asked.

"He controls the team."

Was everything about the flyball team? "Family mattered most to Howard. Bolt is part of your family."

She nodded. "I'm a little emotional. I-I can't believe he's gone." Her voice cracked. I hugged her tight.

Tina's grandmother carried an espresso tray in. The telltale cups stoked my coffee addiction as much as the smell of strong, dark-roasted perfection. I didn't care if the caffeine jolt kept me up all night. She set the tray on the coffee table and left the room.

Tina poured.

"Thank you." I savored the first sip, allowing the earthy flavor to fill my senses. "Can Nonna make coffee for me every day?"

A ghost of a smile broke through Tina's pain. "Her coffee is amazing."

"She's teaching her skills to Joey and Bianca, right?"

"Sometimes I wonder. She scared Howard to death the day he caught her teaching Joey how to chop garlic."

"With a cleaver?"

"Is there another way?"

We shared a cringe. "That is the proper way to chop," I said.

"He was five and the knife blade brushed his elbow."

I managed to stifle my smile. "That's a memory." No wonder Howard had panicked. Humor imparted its gift of healing as Tina and I reminisced. So many memories. Tragedy always reminded me just how close-knit Barkview was.

Finally, Tina asked, "Who killed him, Cat?"

"I don't know." Best to be honest.

"You don't think Rayelle did it?"

I shook my head. "I wish I knew."

"Thank you for that."

"How are Joey and Bianca doing?"

"Joey is quiet like Howard. Bianca doesn't understand why Howard isn't coming to play with her."

I squeezed Tina's hand. "I don't want to interfere or make things worse, but do you think Joey will talk to me?"

"About what?"

"F. Hazing?" Her blank stare didn't give me much hope. "It's something Howard was working on when he was killed."

"Why would Joey know?"

"It could be a word game."

The aha moment ended in fresh tears. "Those games drove Joey crazy. He does speak reasonable Chinese, though. Bianca not as much." Tina glanced at her phone. "Joey needs insulin anyway."

"Joey's a diabetic?"

"Type 1. My brother is, too. Joey was five when he was diagnosed. It's easier to manage now." Tina glanced at her phone. "We had planned on putting him on a pump, but Howard was dead set against it. Said Joey was too young to deal with the tubes. I don't know what's worse. The constant insulin injections or the tubing. The stress he's under right now is an issue. I've had to monitor his sugar often. Thankfully it's all here." She flashed her phone screen.

Graphs and numbers meshed together. "How does it work?" I asked.

"Howard installed an app on my phone that displays real-time readings."

"Does it affect Joey's ability to play soccer?"

"No. He's still amazing." She flushed. "Doesn't bother him. The alarm on my phone goes off if his blood sugar is trending downward." A number flashed green on her phone screen. "His sugar has been controlled since Howard installed the app. Before that, Joey crashed without warning. It's a mother's worst nightmare. Now, my phone alerts me when the trend starts. It also tracks his kidney issues which is a relief."

"I had no idea." I couldn't imagine caring for a child with serious health problems.

"Just one more thing. You get used to it. Nonna reminds me how lucky we are to have the technology. Controlling my brother's sugar about killed my mom. Kids are more adaptable. Howard lost it when Joey was diagnosed."

That made sense. "Two years ago?" The date fit with the F. Hazing documents. Howard would do anything to help his son. Did Howard develop something to test insulin levels? Why would the FBI be involved in that?

Tina typed on her phone. "Joey's on his way. He's happy to help catch the guy who killed his dad."

I savored the last drop of espresso as Joey slid across the tile floor in socks. He grabbed the chair back for an abrupt stop. Bayle dove behind my legs.

"Hey, Mom." A blend of both parents, Joey's dark hair and olive skin were all Tina. The shape of his chin reminded me of a mini-Howard. He'd be a heartbreaker in a couple of years.

"This is Miss Cat. She needs your help figuring out one of your dad's puzzles."

Joey's nod reminded me of Tina. "Okay. What are the letters?"

I wrote F. Hazing on a Post-it.

"*Fang zhi*. Dad said it meant to guard against or protect.'"

Tina and I stared open-mouthed. "You're a genius, Honey." Tina hugged him close.

Joey reached his arms around Tina's waist. "Nah. I made that puzzle up."

"That's cool," I said. "Why?"

"Dad told me this"—He pointed to a small scar on his right shoulder—"would help me control my diabetes. He asked me what I wanted to call it."

"Did he use a needle?" I asked, but I already knew. Howard had injected one of his trackers into his son. Did Tina know her son was a research guinea pig?

CHAPTER 15

My Jag blocked Sean's SUV in J. Tracker's parking lot as he belted JRu into the passenger seat. Talk about meant-to-be timing. I left the engine running and Bayle barking and straining against his seatbelt as I jumped out. "I've been asking questions about Howard." I paused for effect. "Have five minutes?"

Sean glanced at his watch, indecision showing in every on-alert nerve. Not that I blamed him. He'd just been cornered. "For the record, I'm being cooperative," he finally said.

"Thank you." I meant it. No legal reason compelled him to talk to me. Post-its ready, I patted my slacks. Sean handed me a pen from his breast pocket. "Who is F. Hazing?"

Sean's knotted brow aged him considerably more than his thirty-something years. "I don't know."

I laid the Petronics chip drawing on his hood and pointed to the inventor's name. Late afternoon Torrey pine shadows weren't helping any. Sean switched on his phone light. Nose to paper, he scanned the drawing. "Where did you get these?"

"A reporter never reveals her sources."

"Howard." More an observation than a question. I wondered where Sean was going with this. "The drawing looks familiar. Howard designed this while working for J. Tracker. The intellectual property rights belong to me."

"Howard relinquished his rights to the J. Tracker collar royalties for any product development. If he developed this when working for you, then F. Hazing worked for you, too."

"Not necessarily." Sean motioned me to hand over a Post-it and his pen. He scribbled the letters in various orders and then crumpled the paper. "Knowing Howard, it's probably a Chinese anagram." Sean crossed his arms. "But you knew that."

"You knew Howard well."

A regretful head-shake I hadn't anticipated. "I did. I respected him, too. We were roommates at Caltech freshman year. Howard designed and I sold the ideas."

"What happened?" I asked.

"Joey's diabetes changed him. Howard was always too serious. Tina taught him how to enjoy life. After his son's diagnosis, Howard stopped going home. He locked himself in the lab for days on end. A couple of months later, he emerged. Looked like a grizzly who'd discovered the cure for everything known to man."

Had he? "What happened next?"

"He told me about the injectable tracker. I was all in. Figured we'd change the world like we always planned to do in college." No denying the youthful exuberance in Sean's wry smile.

"Except," I said.

"It wasn't commercially viable."

I waited for an exiting car to pass before asking. "Why not?"

"J. Tracker sells dog collars and related consumables. We are not a medical device company."

"Why not partner with a company that is?" Surely there are companies that could help."

"Howard wanted to retain control. He hired Alan Thorpe to explore our options. Even he agreed that a larger, specialized company needed to develop the technology," Sean explained. "I felt like a buzzkill, but I'd told Howard the truth. He went crazy. Even Bolt's persona changed. He acted up in day care. Howard missed meetings. His attitude affected morale. I bought him out six months later."

"How does the injectable work?" I asked.

"I don't know the details." Sean exhaled.

His long pause indicated otherwise. I tapped my foot.

"I'm not evading an answer. I really don't know. Howard was a talented inventor. I do know the scanner is about the size of a grain of rice. It's injected into the scruff of the dog's neck. It's powered by body-generated heat using nanogenerators driven by ultrasonic waves."

"A nano what?"

"Don't ask me. I'm just the sales person."

I believed him. "How do you get the information?"

"The device transmits information to a diagnostic computer through a wifi connection and a Bluetooth connection."

"Would a phone work?"

"Sure. Or a specialized scanner. The injectable Howard proposed to me tracked twenty common disease markers for kidney disease, cancer, diabetes, and heart conditions."

Impressive. I suddenly understood how Sean and Howard worked well together. "Does it work on all, uh, animals?"

Sean's flush confirmed more than his words. "Theoretically. At the time, the liability didn't warrant moving forward."

"The device is a GPS tracker, too, isn't it?"

"Among other things," Sean admitted.

"What other things?"

"Aside from the medical application, it tracked linked devices. Locations. Who the device came in contact with. Exercise patterns. Counted steps. I'm sure there's more. It was a powerful mini-computer."

Talk about major privacy issues. "So, what happened next?"

"Howard threatened to pursue it on his own."

"Did he?"

"I don't know. A couple of years ago the timing wasn't right."

"It is now?"

"Maybe. The world we live in today is all about tracking your location, your buying preferences."

No kidding. How many times did an ad show up on my phone for the same thing I'd searched for earlier?

"I owe it to Howard to see this through for him." His clenched jaw indicated another agenda. "Tina and the kids will be set for life."

They already were. Howard had seen to that. "What has changed? The same obstacles still exist."

"The dog world might be ready for it. There are no government regulations hindering further development in animals. The international community may also be viable. Not in the United States. Imagine what that would mean if we could develop a similar device for humans." Despite his words, I swear his green eyes looked like dollar signs. "Stopping a heart attack before it happened. Diagnosing cancer before it started growing. The list is endless."

"Did Howard work with someone?" I asked.

"He worked best alone. Even Tina knew to back off when he was in a mood."

"Yet she joined your flyball team."

Sean smirked. "Yeah. That was something."

"Howard didn't react the way you expected," I said

"You mean the way Tina expected. I told her Howard had another agenda." Sean shook his head. "He practically drove her to me."

"Maybe Bella is ill," I suggested.

"Two vets say no, but..." Sean scratched his jaw. "If Howard injected Bella, he might have known something we don't."

"Is there even a working prototype?" My nonchalance failed miserably.

"You should never play poker, Cat."

Sound advice. "I have no proof."

"You suspect." Sean took a deep breath.

Time for a subject change. "Rumor has it your business needs a new product."

"Every business needs new products. I'll not deny that the Cavalier dognappings hurt J. Tracker's sales."

"Howard developed your new products when he worked here."

"J. Tracker has a full creative research and development department," Sean insisted.

"You need the injectable..."

Sean chose his words carefully. "I'd like to develop it. At this point, I don't really know if it's viable or not. I'd like to think it is. Truth is, I'll do anything to keep JRu healthy. I get it now."

So did I. Sean might not be as self-serving as I'd feared. Opportunistic, yes. With Howard gone, was this the last great innovation for J. Tracker? Would he kill for it?

CHAPTER 16

I had a pretty good handle on the FBI's involvement now. To tell or not to tell Russ, I debated, as I set the dinner table with copper-woven place mats, wine glasses and fancy lacquered chopsticks.

Who was I kidding? Russ would know the minute he looked into my eyes. Part of me really hated how well he read me when I barely scratched his surface. The other part...

The timer buzzed. I turned off the brown rice. I'd thought about picking up takeout from Nell's, but Bayle's healthy, homemade dinner motivated me to create a spicy Asian stir-fry with veggies I had in the refrigerator and my yummy garlic chili and hoisin mixture.

Bayle had staked out the window seat, his belly seeking the last warming rays. I had to admire his priorities. Eat, chase ball and crash. What more was there in life, anyway?

Suddenly, his head popped up and he barked for a good second before the doorbell rang. Maybe he did possess watchdog traits after all?

"Bayle, quiet." I pointed to the floor. He obeyed. Sort of. He commando-crawled to the door while growling deep in his throat. I stepped over obstacle-Bayle to open the door.

Matata shot through woofing. Fortunately, he leaped high enough to avoid knocking out Bayle, who also jumped to all fours while barking in unison.

Ugh! "Bayle, quiet." Not even a visual acknowledgment. One step forward and two steps backward with this dog. I sighed.

Russ shook a plastic water bottle. Clanking coins stopped both dogs mid-bark. They hit the tile, paws over their ears.

"The command again, Cat," Russ ordered.

No missing that cue. "Bayle, quiet."

"Praise him. Give him a treat."

Forget Russ's greeting. This could be real progress. "Good boy." I took two from my pocket and tossed one to each dog. At this rate, I'd be out by Wednesday. Worse, if Rayelle wasn't released tomorrow, Bayle's prepared food would run out too. I couldn't think about that now.

"Well done." Russ handed me the penny-filled Coke bottle. "This is a good training tool."

I kissed him. "He's supposed to be trained."

"Bayle needs to understand your commands and expectations."

Aunt Char had said the same thing. "How do you know so much about dog training?"

Russ handed me a copy of *Training for Dummies*. I juggled the book and the water bottle, eyeing the bright yellow cover and then him. "Rayelle isn't going to be released anytime soon, is she?"

"No."

Who said I couldn't read him? My gaze locked on Bayle. Fear. No, panic sucked the breath right out of me. Bayle sensed something. His head cocked to the left and he woofed. Not an ear-piercing bark, but a this-can't-be-good bark.

"Will she be charged with murder?" I didn't recognize that squeak as my own voice.

"Officially, it will be interfering with a police investigation."

What a crock of... "She's been cooperating for two days."

Russ shrugged. "Think of it more as time to prove her innocence." He walked into the dining area, pulled the cork out of the chardonnay bottle he'd brought and poured two glasses. "To success."

Whatever that looked like. I took a long swallow. "I don't understand." Not exactly true. Rayelle couldn't be eliminated as a suspect. They had to charge her with something to continue holding her. The ramifications just about knocked me over.

Russ handed me a schoolroom spiral notebook. I recognized the Bichon cartoon cover right away. "Rayelle's recipes."

He nodded. "Bayle's food is marked. There are also instructions for the catering event on Thursday."

I yoga-breathed. There was more.

"Rayelle suggested you host the Sunday segment."

"Me? Prepare dog food?" That had to be a cosmic joke.

"She highlighted the cheddar cheese and turkey bacon treat recipe." He frowned at my crossed arms. "Mix five ingredients, stir, cut, bake."

"With Bayle as my helper and taster?" Odds favored Bayle dissing the treat.

Russ sampled the stir-fry. "This is good. Maybe if you used a Shar-Pei taster?"

Great idea, except the audience responded favorably to Bayle. Did I dare replace him and the hostess? "You're helping me."

Russ didn't even blink. He'd expected my reaction. "A sure way to wiggle your way into Matata's heart."

I wanted to glare, but the dog's lolling pink tongue framed by a semi-sweet chocolate mane tugged at my heart.

Russ gestured to the grocery bag. "Chicken thighs, peas, carrots, and baby spinach. Looks like you made enough brown rice."

Better to have more than not enough. A Wright family motto evident in my waistline.

"We'll try the cheddar cheese and turkey bacon treats, too."

"We'll be up all night."

"Maybe."

A suggestion or a promise?

"Let's eat first. You can tell me what you learned today," Russ suggested.

I plated the meal. Both dogs hugged my heels to the table, which was designed to seat six. We chose two seats across from each other.

Russ's chopsticks clicked with purpose. "Mel's financials show significant cash withdrawals."

Shrimp dropped from my chopsticks to the floor. Matata's ready tongue beat the three second rule. "How much?"

"Three twenty-five-hundred-dollar withdrawals coinciding with losing flyball matches."

"Gambling on flyball? Where do you even find a bookie willing to lay odds?" Fiscally conservative Nell would have a fit.

"You'd be surprised. The last withdrawal occurred the night Mel accused Howard of cheating."

"What did he do?" I could guess.

"Witness says he advised her to prove it. Then he walked away."

No doubt pushing high-strung Mel right over the top. My notes filled six Post-its.

"What did you discover?" Russ asked, too nonchalantly.

"Nothing to top that." Which was true. He'd just handed me a suspect and a possible motive. I'd investigated where he'd asked me not to. "I met with Alan Thorpe."

Russ's chopsticks never paused. "What was your impression?"

"Nothing noteworthy except his link to Trooper TC Security. What do you know about them?" Did Russ flinch? It happened so fast, I couldn't be sure.

"Trooper TC is on my radar. My advice to you is to focus on the money."

A solid suggestion since he'd just shut the door on Trooper TC. Did that make Jen a good guy or a bad guy? Ugh. The secrets were making me crazy. I also knew this was no normal murder.

Surprisingly, Russ didn't press me, changing the subject to all things Barkview until we cleared the table to prep the baking ingredients. Good thing I previewed the recipes before starting preparation. The dough had to chill for an hour before we could roll it out, then cut and bake the treats. Russ chopped. I assembled. Bayle and Matata guarded the entry outside the foot traffic zone with sphinxlike poise.

We completed the spice-less chicken and rice meals with only a short delay opening the supplement capsules. Who knew dogs with stomach problems and dry skin benefited from ginger, Vitamin E, and Omega 3 fish oil?

Rolling out and cookie-cutting the treats proved the most challenging. Not the motions, the focus. As directed, I floured the cutting board, dusting every surface and my hands in ghostly white. Russ tossed me a kitchen towel. I used his black shirt instead, leaving a perfect hand-print on his shoulders. "You're marked for life."

His sexy brow lift drew my attention while he dumped a

man-size handful of flour on my head. It went everywhere. In my ears, up my nose, down my shirt front, flour floated around us in an angelic cloud.

"Fast forward thirty years," Russ remarked.

Never. Aunt Char taught me better. "You should talk, Mr. Ghost of Christmas Past." Not really. His dusted temple appeared far more distinguished than scary.

Matata wasn't so lucky. The Bride of Frankenstein-streak bolting through his mane brought us both to hysterics. Except for paw prints on the floor, Bayle got off unscathed. All considered, the mess was worth it.

Russ slipped the cookie sheet in the oven. "You can do this on Sunday."

"I know. Thanks for the dry run."

"Shower?" Russ suggested.

Was that an invitation?

CHAPTER 17

I dropped Bayle at the Fluff and Buff under Michelle's capable care with only a twinge of guilt and, dare I say, regret? Naturally, Bayle didn't even bat those enviable eyelashes. After three days of constant companionship, I should feel thrilled to be free. Why, then, did I keep glancing toward my empty seat?

I headed south on Third Street and turned onto Sycamore. Set behind the Sit and Stay Café, in a green-gabled carriage house, the BIS Barkery invited customers through an award-winning, stained-glass door depicting flyball mania.

I parked behind the restaurant, away from Nell's big-sis eye. Not that I intended to grill Mel. Okay, maybe I did. Nell in protection mode wasn't going to help anyone.

A welcome bell tinkled my arrival. More country kitchen than Victorian in décor, the barkery's charming gingham curtains and coordinating tablecloths, along with an old-fashioned picnic hamper display, always brought beach barbecues and campouts to mind. The Halloween theme continued with a more whimsical flair. Witch legs poked out of the ground and a cauldron; another witch had crashed into a pole. Various brooms completed the look.

Rolling pin in hand, dressed in a neat black chef's jacket with her flowing auburn hair pulled back in a ponytail, Mel looked like an industrious entrepreneur. Brisbane, her red Aussie, paced at her side.

"As agreed, the biscuits will be ready for pick-up on Thursday by ten," Mel announced.

"No doubt. You're a professional." Mel's emerald eyes darted from me to the door and back, while Brisbane shifted from one foot to the other. Fear or ADHD?

"Thank you for that." She chewed her lip, her rolling pin abandoned. "W-what can I do for you?"

"I'd like to know why you withdrew twenty-five hundred dollars the day before the last three flyball matches against Howard Looc."

"I...uh..." A four-alarm fire burned on her cheeks. "How did you...?"

Clearly not what she expected me to ask. What else was she hiding? I turned my best schoolmarm brow raise on her.

Mel fidgeted. "Nell is gonna kill me. She told me..."

"Told you what?" I felt bad about keeping the pressure up, but half answers weren't working.

"To let it go." Mel and Brisbane paced in unison. "I swear Howard was cheating. There's no way he could've won so often without cheating."

"Unless he had a better team," I suggested.

"He didn't," she announced flatly. "I mean, I don't know how Bayle will change things yet, but individually each dog's time is no better than any of Fur in a Blur's dogs." She wiped her hands on her apron. "At first I thought his ball launcher wasn't to code. His dog's ball time is a tenth of a second faster."

I pulled my Post-its from my pocket and snatched the signing pen from the register cup. "How fast are they?"

She picked up and then set down the rolling pin. "Turns out speed isn't the key. It's the ball arc. Standard machines arc at twenty percent. Howard's are individually calibrated."

"Not against the rules?"

"No. It's pretty ingenious, actually. I fixed that for us. I filmed our team and adjusted the launcher for our dogs."

"So, your engineering degree is paying off?" I asked.

"Not exactly. I cut our time too, but Howard's team still won. I watched his relay system next. His transitions are flawless. I'm still working on that. Next I tested his dog food."

She had my attention. "How did you do that?"

That four-alarm flush notched up. "I, uh, got a sample at the last race."

No doubt when no one was looking. I frowned, but Mel continued, "All of Howard's dogs eat Rayelle's food."

I did a double take. "Since when has Rayelle cooked for the dogs on Howard's team?"

"She doesn't cook for each dog, exactly. She created the recipes a couple of years ago," Mel explained.

"What kind of food?" If Bayle's food was any indicator, the dogs were eating the perfect athlete's diet.

"Nothing earth-shattering. Just nutritious meats and supplements that improve health."

This entire conversation would make a good segment for *Fido's Food Fest*. Still, it was odd that Rayelle hadn't told me.

"I don't want to believe Howard is, I mean was, doping the dogs."

"You mean the supplements?"

"No. BIS adds supplements to our breed-specific treats, too. I mean enhancing drugs like steroids."

No way! Rayelle would never do anything to hurt Bayle. Come to think of it, neither would Howard or Alan.

"Before you say anything, Micky says I was wrong."

Puzzled, I asked, "Who's Micky?"

"The PI I hired."

"You hired a private investigator to test Howard's flyball team's food?" So that's what the money had been for.

Mel's stance just dared me to judge. Even Brisbane eyed me. "Yeah. What other choice did I have?"

Train more. Recruit faster dogs. The cheating go-to bothered me. "Maybe Howard just has a better system," I suggested.

Mel huffed. "Rumor has it Bayle is a ringer." Her impatience ruled. "How fast is he?"

"What's fast?"

"A 2.2 second run."

I shrugged. No need to feign confusion with my flyball know-how.

"Where is he?"

"At the Fluff and Buff."

"You were there yesterday."

Why it even mattered escaped me. "He's a Bichon." What more needed to be said?

It took a second, but she got it. "Oh, right."

"Is that why you're pranking Rayelle? So she'll leave town and not compete?"

Mel glanced at her gloved hands. "Not exactly. I don't trust her."

"Why not?" Maybe jealousy wasn't the driver.

"She's a-a..." Mel's eyes slitted. This wasn't going to be good. Post-it pad ready, I watched Mel's lips twitch, searching for the right word. "A sleazy home-wrecker."

That was on point. I cleared my throat, trying hard not to crack a smile. "Uh, why do you say that?"

"I overheard Howard and Tina arguing at the flyball park two weeks ago. Howard said, '*Enough. The decision has been made. We're moving on.*'"

Mel's Cheshire-cat smirk indicated there was more. "Tina responded, '*You're willing to destroy our family for her?*'"

Hooked, I sucked in my breath. Tina's interpretation of the event varied considerably. There had to be more. "And?"

"The next day Bayle replaced Bella."

Flyball again. I should've guessed.

"I won't prank again. I know Alan Thorpe is a good coach, too. He's really smart." Was that another blush?

"Send me Micky's contact info and Nell need never know."

"Know what?" Nell glided through the back entrance sideways.

"I think Mel should challenge Alan Thorpe to a chess game," I said quickly. Whew. Talk about close.

"That's a great idea. Mel is always looking for a game," Nell agreed.

"That can be arranged." Mel returned to rolling the dough.

"If you plan to ask Mel to fill in on *Fido's Food Fest*, she's too busy," Nell announced.

I owed Nell big time for that gloss-over. "I understand."

Mel didn't. She started to speak twice. I cut her off before the third try. "I will fill in."

Their jaws dropped in unison. "You?" Mel sputtered.

"I can cook." Defensiveness just came out.

"Really? You've never met a recipe you can follow, my friend," Nell said.

"I can so." I'd even done it last night.

"Don't forget your lack of acting skills," Nell added.

"Acting? I'm showing the audience how to cook dog treats."

"You're selling dogs living a healthy lifestyle to dog lovers," Nell said.

Denial died on my lips. Talk about drilling down past that special undefinable something that made any show successful. It wasn't about the camera loving Rayelle. Her passion for dogs and their care—of which I had zero—drove the show's success. Omg. What was I thinking?

CHAPTER 18

I think best when I'm in the shower or walking, so I contemplated my options during the block-and-a-half stroll past spooky Victorians to police headquarters. Could I conjure any kind of passion for baking dog treats? Finding Howard's killer in the next five days promised to be less daunting.

Thanks to Mel, Tina, the wronged wife, now topped my suspect list. Rayelle's secrets still bothered me plenty. Why hadn't she told me she'd developed the nutrition plan for Howard's flyball team? The act itself wasn't particularly suspicious. Stephan, the convenient old flame, Sean, the rival ex-partner, and Alan, the second in command, all jumbled together with no hands-down suspect leader.

I waved to the receptionist and walked into the buzzing bullpen, as the chief fondly referred to the officers' cubicle area. Any hope Russ could assist me vanished the moment I saw Uncle G's closed door. I waved at Officer Richie lounging outside the break room door and pointed toward Uncle G's office.

Richie's grimace said more than his head shake. Retreat

seemed prudent until Richie gestured for me to follow him to an interrogation room. "Russ said you'd be coming by to see the enhanced Bichon Bisquets security footage. He apologizes for not being available."

No apology needed for the effective way in which Russ had cleared my visit. The aseptic starkness of the room upped my stress level, undoubtedly as intended for any unfortunate visitor. Richie offered me a chair alongside his in front of a portable keyboard and extra-large monitor mounted on a utilitarian metal stand. His keystrokes echoed as he loaded the video.

Post-its ready, I felt for the pen I'd tucked behind my ear, the one I'd forgotten to return from the BIS Barkery. Guilt swamped me the second I saw the logo, probably also intended by the environment. I covered the contraband logo with my thumb.

Richie and I watched the video once through. The enhancement had helped a little. The blob still looked like a pixelated apparition with no real defining features or shape.

"Tech thinks the blob could be a reflection of a metallic cape."

Or someone dressed in a reflective sweat suit with a hat. "Can you skip back to the envelope drop-off and pause?"

"Sure. What are you looking for?" Richie asked.

I held my phone up to the screen. "Is this the same dog?" Comparing BB's photo with the wolf image delivering the envelope resolved nothing. The images looked similar. "You have more experience than I do. What do you think?"

Officer Richie scratched his scruffy strawberry-blondish stubble. Why that look raged in Hollywood, I'd never get. "I don't know."

Without a frontal facial view, I didn't either. "Can you play the Ciao Bella surveillance?"

Richie glanced at his watch, then toward the door, and quickly uploaded the file. "No one goes in or out the front, side, or roll-up back door after closing. The perimeter alarm was set at 10:55. No windows or doors were opened until Mrs. Looc carried Bianca to her car parked out back at 12:15 a.m." Richie rubbed the knot above his eye. "Poor lady. The chief and I met her at her house at 1:30 a.m."

"No footage inside the kitchen?" I asked.

"No." He pointed out Tina and her mother locking the front door at eleven and leaving at 12:15. "Mrs. Looc's grandmother is upstairs with the kids. The children kissed Tina goodnight at 8:30 p.m."

Tina's alibi was her mother. "Could Tina have left the kitchen?"

He shook his head.

"Who is the security company?" I asked.

"Trooper TC. They have been cooperative."

I watched the footage anyway. The marine layer had rolled in, casting an eerie haze over the gabled porch. Not even a breeze stirred near the garbage cans.

"Any visitors for Tina?"

"Mrs. Looc met Stephan McCarthy at the receiving entrance at 9:09."

"Can I see that?"

Richie tapped on the keyboard. Sure enough, at 9:09 Stephan's Bug chugged up to the roll-up door in back. A few minutes later, Tina lifted the door. They spoke for five minutes before she handed him a narrow package. Was it long enough to be a knife? Tina's shoulder blocked his reaction. Next, Stephan's kiss grazed Tina's cheek as she glanced at her phone. Almost immediately, she hurried back inside. The timing collaborated with Stephanie's statement regarding her brother's arrival at The Frosty Pups.

"Did Stephan contact Tina prior to stopping by?"

"He texted her." Richie loaded another file. "Text read *I'm ready. Are you?*"

"Ready for what?"

"Mrs. Looc and Stephan separately confirmed the text pertained to a Blue Bay puppy Stephan is adopting." Richie pointed to a picture of a fluffy, sleepy-eyed puppy. "About time he's ready to move on," Richie remarked. "Can't imagine going three years dogless."

Three years with no responsibility? On the surface it all looked innocent, but could Stephan and Tina have been conspiring? "What was in the package?"

"A silver collar for the puppy. I confirmed with the Posh Pup that Mrs. Looc purchased a silver collar engraved with Lady B."

"That's the puppy's name?" Maybe it was as innocent as Uncle G believed. "Can I see Rayelle?"

"Uh..." Richie stretched his neck, glancing at the camera.

Clearly not chief-approved. Richie needed convincing. "I need to talk to her about flyball practice. You know, I'm taking Bayle for his first team run tonight."

"Is he really the ringer they say he is?" Richie asked.

"Who is 'they?'"

"Everyone."

Kill me if I ever got on the Barkview gossip train. "He's fast." Which wasn't a lie. "You should come see for yourself."

Richie smiled. "I just might. Stay here. No one told me not to let you see her."

He disappeared, leaving the Ciao Bella surveillance video on screen. Intentional, accidental or just good luck? Who knew? I copied the file to my emergency thumb drive and folded my hands on the interrogation table. Rayelle arrived ten minutes later. To my relief, she wore knee-torn jeans and a familiar blue peasant blouse.

I expected smiles, not a near-panicked "Where's Bayle?"

"He's fine. I dropped him at the Fluff and Buff."

"The morning before practice?"

Like that meant something to me. "He needed to be brushed."

Rayelle flopped into the chair opposite me, her forehead basketed in her hands. "It's okay. I'm sorry. I know he's a little high maintenance."

"A little? Last night, Russ and I cooked..."

Her gaze teased mine. "All night, I hope."

"I...uh..." I blushed. So, she had set me up with Russ. I should be mad. Yet I responded to Rayelle's good old mischievous smile with my own.

"I know you are doing the best you can. Bayle will need to go back to the Fluff and Buff tomorrow."

"That's fine." She'd find out about the daily appointments soon enough. Better get to it. "Why didn't you tell me you created the diet for Howard's dogs?"

Her confusion had to be genuine. "Ward and I talked about dog nutrition the first time we met. When he asked me for some recipes he could make at home, I never thought he'd actually do it. Frankly, I didn't think it was important."

Sounded innocent enough. An openness lecture seemed petty, but I had to start getting ahead of these issues. "It's something you did with the guy you're accused of murdering. You'd better believe it's important. So, is there any other seemingly insignificant action that has occurred between you two?"

She glanced at the cameras. "Barkview thinks Ward and I were lovers, don't they?"

I nodded. No sense sugarcoating the truth. "Why didn't you tell me about the puppy?"

"What puppy?"

"Howard left you Bolt's offspring."

She fell back in the chair. "Omg! He did breed him after all. I didn't know. You have to believe me."

"Your eyes say innocent, your body language not so much."

Rayelle jumped to her feet and paced. "You could always read me. Right after Tina went to Sean's team, Howard told me he had a plan for the next generation. He was impressed with the way I'd trained Bayle and wanted me to work with any new additions. He didn't share details. This does not look good for me, does it?"

What could I say? Reasonable as it sounded, her motives just mounted.

Rayelle ran her fingers down her hair. "There were a few unusual incidents that happened in the shop. Ward told me not to worry, but I'm not so sure now. The day after I opened, Miss Rodeo Drive came in carrying a Chihuahua in her purse and ordered a box of biscuits. She sat at the table by the window feeding the dog for thirty minutes and left. Ward strolled in a minute later and sat at the same table. Not so interesting except the lady left an envelope on the table. It wasn't there when I bused it after Ward left. It happened again last week."

"Same woman?" I asked.

"Yes."

"What did she look like?"

"A fashion week junkie."

Rayelle's quips always made me smile. "Specifically."

"She was a statuesque Latina. Maybe thirtyish. No wedding ring, but she wore a honking pair of diamond earrings."

"Antique diamonds?" Could the diamond Bayle found be hers?

"No. Nouveau riche sparkle-studs."

Dead end on the diamond. Why an envelope? Was Howard using Bichon Bisquets as a drop? For what? "You confronted Howard?"

"You bet. He made some lame excuse about the previous tenants."

"You didn't push it?"

She shook her head. "In retrospect, I should have. The thing is, Ward hated to be questioned. He got downright ornery about it."

Traits of a man accustomed to getting his way for sure. No doubt reminiscent of Tina's issues with her own overbearing father. "So, you just let it slide?"

"It was easier and didn't seem like a biggy at the time."

I got why she'd done it. Selling that to Uncle G and Russ would be difficult.

"I don't know how much time we have left, but you'd better get your Post-its ready. I need to prepare you for tonight's flyball practice. First of all, wear noise-canceling headphones. The barking will put you right over the top."

I froze. "Barking?" That squeak couldn't be my voice. "How many dogs will be there?"

"It's not so much the quantity but the hyper-excited pitch."

Maniacal barking dogs. I hadn't signed up for this. Rayelle's hand covered mine. "You'll be fine. Bayle needs you. And so do I."

I knew that.

"You'll need to prep Bayle."

Another wave of anxiety set in. Post-its ready. "Prep him?"

"Feed him at 4 p.m. Walk him..."

Seven Post-its later, an athlete's training program I could only admire emerged. "You really want me to slick back his head fur? I mean, this is only practice." Swimmers oiled their bodies for meets, but a dog?

Rayelle exhaled. "This is his *grande entrée.* He must live up to the hype."

"Hype?" There was more to this, I could tell.

"Ward expected Bayle to shake up the flyball world and force every team to up their game. I suspect more spectators will attend tonight's practice than attended the last ten meets combined."

Her enthusiasm drew my smile. I didn't ask for a head count. How many people could that possibly be, anyway?

"Ward envisioned flyball as a televised sport."

"Dreaming is a good thing." No wonder she'd gone along with Howard's plans. In the end, I had Howard to thank for enticing her to Barkview.

Painful as that was to admit, I got her point. "Bayle needs to shine tonight. What else do I need to know?"

She demonstrated the proper chest hold at the relay start. She lost me with the ball-on-a-string finish, but I nodded anyway. Alan would shepherd me through the process.

"I know you're not a picture taker, but could you take a picture of Bayle for me?" Rayelle's voice cracked.

"Sure." I hugged her close. I may not qualify as a flyball aficionado, but I'd been around enough dog people to get that Rayelle's baby faced a milestone without her. "I'll take care of him."

"I know you will. You're the best, sis."

With any luck I'd get through this and stay in the family.

CHAPTER 19

The fur was flying when I arrived at Tina's doorstep. Dogs barked, Bianca wailed, and Tina shrieked with ear-piercing splendor, all through the solid walnut door. I massaged my temples with no luck. My head still pounded. Later seemed the prudent plan.

I about-faced, intent on flight, until a green-striped soccer jersey slipping out the door caught my eye. Add khakis, and Joey stoically standing there looked so like Howard that I couldn't help but stop.

"I didn't ring the doorbell."

"We have a Bolt bell."

Of course. Without the heavy door's barrier, Tina's next eardrum-rupturing screech caused us to wince in unison.

Joey pulled the door closed. "Mom's busy. Will you take me to my friend's house?"

I wanted to say no. I knew less about kids, never mind grieving kids, than I did about dogs. One blink from his teddy-bear-brown eyes and I folded. Watch out, girls. The kid had heartbreaker covered.

"You'd better ask your mom's permission first." Part of me hoped she'd refuse.

His eyebrows shot up. "Fine." Joey's fingers flew across the phone, faster than even Sandy's, if that was possible. A second later, the phone pinged. He flashed the screen in my direction. "She says okay and thank you. She'll pick me up in a few hours."

So much for escape. "Do you have everything?"

Joey eyed the door and held up his phone. Couldn't blame him for not wanting to go back inside or dogging my heels as if afraid I'd somehow leave without him.

I opened the SUV's door and motioned him inside. Joey picked a small sand dollar off the passenger seat before sliding in.

"You took Bayle to the beach?" His interest seemed odd.

"No. I swear that dog's tail collects junk. I have no idea where he picked that up."

"Bolt is like that, too. Bianca's tootsie rolls look like rabbit turds on his chest."

Spoken like a true nine-year-old, snicker and all. The candy mat visual struck my funny bone, too.

"Where's Bayle?" Joey asked.

"At the Fluff and Buff."

"Why?" No malice. Just confusion in his frown.

"He needed to be groomed." My tone lacked confidence.

"Right before a race?"

"Yeah. He needs to look..." Joey's skepticism really bothered me. "You can't be serious. Who slicks back a dog's hair to play flyball?"

"The winning team."

"Come on." I wasn't giving in that easily.

"Aerodynamically..." I should've known. Mini-Howard droned on and on.

Surrender my only option, I held up my hand. "Okay. Okay, I get it." I really didn't, but enough already. I mean, how much difference could it make?

"You know the real reason, right?" I saw Tina in his mischievously arched brow. "It's really funny to look at."

Hazing! I knew it. I didn't respond. Just zigzagged down the Terraces' hillside per the GPS's instructions.

"Where exactly does your friend live?" I asked as I turned onto the southbound freeway ramp out of Barkview.

Joey typed something on his phone. "Precisely 32.994 degrees north, 117.1912 degrees west."

"That's precise." What else could I say? Another smile crept out despite my best efforts. "Did you meet your friend at school?"

Joey nodded. "He sits next to me in mechanical science."

"Are you in college already?" What were they teaching K-6 kids now?

"I'm in fourth grade. It's a special math and science school. We analyze drawings and how things work."

No wonder Howard had decided against a traditional Barkview education and sent his son to what sounded like an inventor's nirvana. "What's your friend's name?"

"Marcos Ramirez Hernandez III."

"The third? Sounds important." Why did parents do that to kids? I'd suffered my fair share of adolescent teasing, being named after a coastal California island. My kids would be named something simple like Charlotte after my aunt or... Russ's bright blue eyes, a crib, and a jungle blanket scattered my focus.

"You okay?" Joey asked. "You're all red."

Of course, my cheeks were burning. I sputtered the first words to come to mind. "So, is your friend's dad an inventor, too?"

"No. Marcos says he's an important man in Mexico. He doesn't see him a lot."

"That's sad."

"I know. His mom says he's safer here. His dad comes to visit."

Kidnappings were not unusual in Mexico. Thanks to men and women like Russ, kids could be kids in America.

We drove in silence past a few Rancho Santa Fe horse estates until the GPS directed me to a video-monitored gate. High walls blocked any interior view from the street, except for the swaying branches of mesquite trees beyond. Talk about seclusion. I stopped at the security box and pressed the call button. "Hi. I'm dropping Joey Looc off to see Marcos."

"Master Hernandez is expecting him. Drive through. Security will escort you to the house." The gate swung open, revealing an enormous Mediterranean villa reminiscent of one I'd visited on my last sojourn at Lake Cuomo. A terra-cotta roof topped an earth-toned structure framed by a veranda with white pillars. Tranquil tree-shaded gardens could be glimpsed around the corners of the house.

A black SUV blocked the driveway five hundred feet from the palazzo fountain dominating the circular drive. A prize-fighter, judging by his crooked nose and steroid-enhanced upper body, lumbered to my door. The black-on-black uniform brought scary to a new level. "Good afternoon, ma'am. We need to check your car."

I wanted to ask for what, but the purest midnight-black dog I had ever seen approached. At first, I thought it was a Blue Bay Shepherd. On closer inspection, I noted a slightly more wolfish facial structure and brown-black eyes so dark they blended into the fur.

"The dog is beautiful. I've never seen anything like it."

"It's a Black German Shepherd," Joey said. "Marcos isn't even allowed to pet them."

A sin in Howard's son's book for sure. "They have more than one?"

"Three. What's the point of a dog you can't play with?"

No kidding. This dog was no pet. The at-attention stance and purposeful stride reminded me of Max and Maxine when they were on the clock. No wonder we hadn't seen BB's striking blue eyes in the surveillance video. This dog had dropped the envelope.

I followed the handler as the dog sniffed my car in my rearview mirror. A residential bomb search? Who was Marcos's father?

"Joey, does Marcos have diabetes like you?"

His nod brought the pieces together. "You said you met Marcos in mechanical science class?" I asked.

"Well, really at the nurse's office."

"She gives you both insulin shots?"

"Yup. Marcos has a pump now, but it's not right all the time. My dad didn't think I was ready to have one. Mom does. What do you think?"

"I think your parents need to decide." A cop-out answer for sure. What was Howard's deal with the pump? Joey seemed mature enough to handle it. "Does his mom help manage the insulin with her phone?"

"Yup. My dad helped her."

Of course Howard had. Was it at the FBI's request? "What school do you attend?"

"La Jolla Academy."

I called Sandy as soon as I turned back onto the freeway. Call me paranoid, but the guards in my rearview mirror scared me more than my immediate desire for information.

"Hey Boss, I was just about to call you. I got something on Trooper TC," Sandy told me.

"I've got something, too." I filled her in on my suspicions.

"Geez. You said the kid's name is Marcos Ramirez Hernandez III? That's a mouthful." Oddly, the clicking keyboard strokes comforted me. Answers were forthcoming, I knew it.

"Hmm. He attends La Jolla Academy?" Sandy asked.

"According to Joey." I exited the freeway at First Street and turned toward downtown, oddly comforted.

"Pooh. This firewall is…" Sandy, technically stumped?

"A deterrent for smart kids with too much time on their hands." I pictured her crooked grin.

"Nailed that one. I'll call you when I have something."

"No doubt." Sandy never let me down. "What did you find on Trooper TC?"

"F. Hazing is the company founder."

No missing that bomb. "So, Howard founded Trooper TC?" I really should've known.

"Appears so. For the record, there is no real Trooper Tom Collins. The guy on the web page is an actor. Oddly, F. Hazing is currently not a company principal. That's why it took so long to get the info."

"Is Alan Thorpe associated with the company?"

"*Lana Pother* is the technology officer."

Another anagram. No question about it. Alan had known far more than he'd admitted.

My Google watch flashed 2 p.m. Just a few hours until flyball practice. Thanks to Bayle, I'd have Alan's full attention there.

CHAPTER 20

Rayelle had flat-out lied to me. Flyball did not showcase dog athleticism. It sanctioned an ear-piercing barkfest. Yipping, yapping, howling, growling, and woofing in dueling octaves sliced through me, and I was still cocooned inside my road-silent Jaguar.

Bayle wasn't helping any, either. He strained against his seat restraint, his tail hummingbird-fluttering, anticipation visible in every at-attention muscle. Ready for what, I didn't want to know. Instead, I focused on a quick turnaround in the parking lot's roundabout.

Alan crushed any fleeting escape plan. Much as I wanted to escape, that blood-red-and-silver striped jersey made him impossible to miss. Never mind that he and Hawn bodily blocked my accelerating vehicle.

I rolled down my window at his signal. "Good evening, Cat," he said. "Glad you could make it."

More like relieved since he stopped clenching his jaw. Silence seemed prudent. What could I say, anyway?

"Turnout is even better than expected." His cat-got-the-canary grin was getting right under my skin. Any doubt he'd orchestrated this fiasco vanished.

"There's, uh, no parking." A lame excuse, for sure.

"Tsk, never figured Barkview's resolute reporter for a quitter." Alan's dark gaze dared argument.

Resolute reporter? Not exactly flattering. Taking issue made even less sense. He had my number and we both knew it.

Tasting victory, Alan's smile could've passed for magnanimous. "Nothing to fear."

Fear wasn't the problem. I twisted my scarf, my neck tingling in too-vivid remembrance. More like terror. Rational me knew Barkview's pampered pooches weren't go-for-the-throat killers, but still my head went to that dark, dank place, deep in the dog-fighting den. Every bark exacerbated the desperation restricting my breath.

I should have accepted Sandy's offer to come with me, but Aunt Char was on the air and I was a big girl. Or so I thought. Too bad the relaxation techniques I'd practiced seemed out of reach. The panic attack thundered on until I saw Russ leaning against Alan's vehicle, dressed in a navy golf shirt and khakis. His nonchalant attitude, as well as his reassuring grin, calmed me considerably. Suddenly, the flyball practice felt like nothing worse than a dreaded root-canal visit. I clicked on my noise-canceling headset. Not total silence, but the steady hum cut the edge off the barking overload.

It didn't even bother me that Russ promptly faded into the crowd with only a knowing nod. That he'd anticipated my anxiety was enough. He had a job to do here, too. Later we'd meet to compare notes.

For now, I followed Alan's reaperish forefinger beckon toward an orange cone and a motorcycle blocking the parking spot alongside his Escalade.

Alan motioned a slouchy figure decked out in black leather

to pull out. Heavy silver chains clanked as she motored by. I'd expected a motorcycle roar, not a *putter-putter* backfire. I jumped. I wasn't the only one staring, I realized, as the girl with glassy brown eyes took my measure as her bike squeezed by my driver's-side mirror. Who was she? I quickly took a video, more to get the license number, just in case, and pulled into the parking spot.

Alan went right for the passenger side and unbuckled Bayle, effectively ending any sudden dart for freedom. A gracious winner, he handed me Bayle's leash. At least I thought it was happy-go-lucky Bayle until what felt like an Iditarod-caliber Husky about jerked my arm off. My yelp did no good. Mush-dog Bayle dragged me toward the LED-lit sports track. We quick-stepped it through the freshly trimmed grass, past the red-roofed octagonal pavilion where bands played in the summer, to a crowd-lined track reminiscent of Rose Bowl Eve on Colorado Boulevard. Even the canine contingent was dressed in team colors.

"You can't be serious," I muttered.

Alan smiled. "Flyball is big business in Barkview."

No kidding. That odd strip of asphalt whose use I'd never understood had been transformed into two one-hundred-yard racing lanes, each with a series of four jumps separated by glowing barriers, leading to those all-too-familiar mechanized ball boxes.

Clusters of ball-gnawing Australian Shepherds mingled with pacing Greyhounds and prancing Jack Russells, all wound so tight, their adrenalin-fueled barking broke noise ordinances.

No distraction fazed Bayle. He pulled even harder on the leash.

"I see you've prepared Bayle," Alan smiled. Naturally, Hawn heeled perfectly, seeming unaffected by the edgy chaos.

If he meant that I'd Fonzied the puff off him, then yes. Actually, Michelle had done it, but only after an accusatory finger shake that named me the worst dog babysitter ever. He'd gone from fluffy cloud to a gel-slicked, pink-skinned guinea pig in two seconds.

Can a dog get in a huff? I swear Bayle threw his head and snorted at me. Not that I blamed him; he looked ridiculous. Even after Joey's explanation, if Rayelle hadn't insisted, I'd never have done it. I mean, how much faster could he possibly run? I didn't care what the internet said about improved swim times after full body shaving. This was a dog on land.

I was going to find out, I realized. Bayle's swagger reminded me of Renny's champion-dog-show walk. This was Bayle's world. I was only here for the ride.

I waved to Sean Riley huddled with his Jack Russell team, all dressed in suspicious silver-metallic jerseys featuring a holographic J. Tracker logo. Could the video blob have been Sean in flyball attire? Maybe the two men had met and Sean lost his temper? Their sordid history could be viewed as a prosecutable motive. Sean's sidelong perusal of Bayle did nothing to alleviate my doubts. I swear Sean all but snarled at me—or maybe it was at Bayle and I'd gotten in the line of fire.

Bayle acknowledged nothing. His single-minded trek continued. Alan and Hawn followed a step behind, undoubtedly to prevent me from bolting.

Nell greeted us with a smile and a head scratch for Bayle, who avoided her touch altogether. Mel spun in place, her messy bun spilling fire down her rose-tinted jersey. "Pretty big for his fur, I see."

Valid point. This ultra-cool dude seemed too much like James Dean to be goofy Bayle. Mel's evil eye made even less sense. I got her competitive spirit. But did playing head games work on a dog?

Bayle curtailed my lingering with a sharp yank in Bolt's direction. He promptly broke free from Tina's grip and streaked across the two racing lanes, his leash skipping along the pavement. Tina looked like a caricature of a madwoman, with her dark hair floating around her face and her team jersey slipping off one shoulder as she shrieked unheeded commands in his wake.

Bayle sniffed skyward, resisting my dive to safety. Front paws extended, Bolt skidded to a halt barely two inches from full collision. A nod and a mutual butt sniff later and even Tina realized the dogs were BFF's. Her eat-crap-and-die glare drew Bayle's *Huh?* woof.

"They're dogs, Tina," I reminded her. Don't even ask how I figured out Bayle's demeanor.

"Who apparently know more than I do about what was going on." Jealousy, pure and simple, stormed in her dark-as-night eyes. If Howard hadn't already been dead, he'd have been running for his life now.

Alan saw it, too. "We are all teammates, Tina. If you intend to handle Bolt, you'd best remember that."

Another black-and-white-blotched Border Collie nosed into the pack, ending further discussion. She was followed by a wiry woman with knowing hazel eyes.

"Hi. I'm Jen Russo." Her tawny hair pulled back in a neat twist seemed to come alive in the red-and-silver striped Outfoxing Pi jersey. "This is Roxie, the fourth dog on the team." I extended my hand. "Nice to meet you." I'd expected a spit-and-polish army officer, not an easygoing dog-lover.

"I love your aunt's show. Rush home every evening to watch it."

I couldn't help but respond to Jen's contagious fan-smile. I liked her. "You served with the chief?"

"With a friend of the chief's."

That explained her excellent character references. "You were military police?"

"EDC handler."

She read my blank look.

"Sorry. Military acronym. Explosive detection canine handler."

That made sense. Her nothing-but-the-facts answers still set off alarm bells. "Trooper TC trains bomb-sniffing dogs?"

"Today's security needs are multifaceted." She scratched Roxie's head. "Crazy world we live in, huh, girl?"

"Tell me about it," I said.

"Trained her from a pup. The chief introduced me to Howard. She's got the right stuff."

No doubt.

"Roxie will run third today."

Did running order matter? Her frown indicated as much. "Was Roxie the last dog until Bayle's arrival?"

"Yes." She blinked. "Flyball is a team sport. Points are awarded for team performance only. I'm happy to have Bayle on board."

I wanted to believe her, but I still wondered as I watched her lead Roxie away. A military dog handler could be a stellar suspect in a knife attack.

"Roxie is solid. I added her to the team a year ago," Alan explained.

"Is she mad that Bayle replaced Roxie?"

"Bayle replaced Bella." His reference to Tina came through clear enough.

"In the cleanup spot, I mean?"

Alan frowned. "Flyball is a team sport. As in any other team sport, positions change based on performance and strategy. Tonight Bayle will run fourth. Next week we will try him at another spot. Strategy is determined by the competition. Jen knows that."

Made sense, I guess. Pickleball, my preference, wasn't a relay sport. "I meant to ask you about Lana Pother."

I expected guilt, or surprise at the least. Alan didn't even blink. "That's a Russ question," he said so softly that I barely heard him over the roar.

Which confirmed Alan was no innocent.

"I'll take Bayle from here," Alan said.

Not a prayer. I'd promised Rayelle I'd look after Bayle. The dog stayed with me. "Rayelle showed me how to set Bayle." I flinched under his penetrating stare.

"And the release timing?" Alan's look had skeptical schoolmarm covered.

I nodded unconvincingly, based on Alan's clenched jaw reaction.

"The timing is crucial. A fraction of a second can change a win to a loss," he explained.

No pressure there. "It's only practice. It won't affect points." Listen to me repeating Rayelle's insight.

His eyes flashed with ... anger? Disappointment? I wasn't sure. "I'll show you." He motioned for me to follow him.

I did, despite my budding annoyance. A scene solved nothing. Seriously, how hard could it be?

It was more complicated than I'd expected, I realized, seeing Tina crouched on one knee with Bolt's long hind legs balanced on her other.

"Show me," Alan ordered.

I swallowed. One eye on Tina, I knelt and copied her position. At least I thought I did until Bayle's leg slipped off my thigh and he tumbled sideways into a heap. He jumped to all fours, shook, and blinked at me.

"What the...?" Alan's finger jerk almost tugged out his remaining hair.

Jen stepped between us. "I got this. Get Hawn ready." Talk about calmness under duress. Even the surrounding chaotic roar paused, waiting. Alan's glare cut deep into my back, but he walked away.

"Thank you," I said.

"It's not you. Anytime T is around, he's jumpy."

"Who's T?"

"Alan's daughter, Tiffany. She's a piece of work. She drove the motorcycle that saved your parking place. She's hanging on to her motocross position by a thread. Rumor has it she's headed back to rehab."

That explained the glassy-eyed glare. "This"—I gestured around us—"is crazy."

"Yeah. Howard is going to haunt Alan for this fiasco."

Interesting. "I thought Howard wanted a world-class team."

"He did. Howard was a planner. He wanted everything just right," Jen explained.

"Did Alan disagree on the team's direction?"

"More like a difference in marketing strategies. Alan wanted to accept sponsorships and grow the sport through YouTube and TV. Howard wanted a more organic growth."

"They were arguing?" I asked.

Based on Jen's head shake, I'd gotten that one wrong. "Howard never raised his voice. Frankly, the chief's deep-freeze stare doesn't even come close to Howard's."

The recipient of my fair share of Uncle G's stares, I swallowed hard. "Alan wanted results now," I said.

The man had given up his team and gone all-in with Howard. Did Alan need money, too? Rehab for his daughter wouldn't be cheap. With any luck, Sandy's exceptional computer skills could fill in the blanks.

"Don't we all want instant results? Hey. Don't worry about Bayle. You two will be fine." Jen's smile coaxed out mine. "The goal is to create starting blocks for Bayle to push off."

I shook off the conversation. "With my legs?"

"Yeah."

"I copied Tina…"

"Bayle's legs are shorter than Bolt's." She pointed to my thighs. "You need to be lower."

Lower? My muscles already burned. Clearly, I wasn't as fit as I'd thought.

Jen accurately read my blank stare. She crouched beside me and set Bayle on her thighs. "It's geometry, really. Think about how a rabbit can go from stopped to sprint in just a few seconds. It's the bend in their hind legs."

Analogy not working. Apparently, my spatial conception skills needed work.

"Let me make this easier." She removed a tennis ball from her jacket pocket and placed it between my calf and hamstrings. She stepped back and assessed her work. "Not enough. I need something thicker. I'll be right back."

Jen scooted away. Russ's breath tickled my ear. "This will work."

I almost tipped over as he replaced the tennis ball with a rolled towel. "Jen can adjust the angle."

"Thanks." I meant it. Even I knew Bayle needed to do well today.

"Great idea, Russ." Jen's tone indicated a more than passing familiarity with him.

"You know each other?" I asked.

Russ's nod to Jen said it all as he disappeared into the crowd. As she adjusted the towel, she replied, "Chief introduced me to Russ a few months ago. He needed information for an investigation he's working on."

No doubt to do with Marcos Ramirez Hernandez III.

Her wink messed with my composure. "He's a good catch."

"Uh. He is." I had to be tomato-red with that admission.

"Good. Don't let him go." Jen bent over and set Bayle's hind feet on my thigh. I saw it then: a gun holstered in the small of her back. Rather, the outline of a gun. No one carried a concealed weapon in California except criminals and law enforcement. I doubted a dog trainer qualified under San Diego County's rigorous rules. Was Jen working with the chief and Russ, or Howard's murderer?

My gaze searched out Russ to no avail. He'd blended in somewhere.

"You okay?" Jen asked.

"Who are you really?" The words just spilled out. So much for subtlety.

Jen patted my arm. "You're safe, Cat. I'm the person who will get you through this."

Oddly, I believed her. "There's more?"

Her laugh wasn't funny. "Consider yourself to be in the crash course."

"Crash and burn, you mean?"

"Not if I can help it. I'll cue your release. When I swing the ball, let Bayle go." Jen pendulum-swung a tennis ball attached to a colorful five-foot rope. "Bayle will do the rest."

I believed her. Bayle's tense body relaxed as his eyes hypnotically followed the ball. Rayelle had not properly prepared me. Not that I would have retained it all. Who knew a dog relay race could be so complicated? Or that the woman I followed might be more than she seemed?

"First heat is about to start. Watch," Jen ordered.

As if I could look away. Suddenly, a green light flashed and two dogs took off. Both sailed over the jumps, Nell's long-legged black lab outpacing Sean's smaller Jack Russell, until they banked off the box. The second set of dogs, waiting at the same starting line for the first dog to cross, surged forward before I could blink, followed shortly thereafter by the third and four dogs. Mel's Australian Shepherd nosed out their competition at the breath-holding, photo finish.

"We'll do better," Jen announced. "Come on. Our turn."

Better? The hype. The anticipation. Everything was over in twenty-five seconds. Alan was right. Seconds mattered. Heck, split seconds mattered. If I messed up the launch or didn't release Bayle in time...

"Stop worrying. You'll do fine," Jen assured me. "Bayle knows what to do."

The last time I'd taken my aunt's Cavalier into the show ring, she'd managed just fine without me. Hopefully, Bayle wouldn't need me either. I set up as instructed. My heart pounded as I waited.

Red light. Yellow light. Green.

Like a bullet, Bayle shot right out of my grip. I jumped to my feet, watching him not even break stride as he glided effortlessly over the jumps. He hit the ball launcher in perfect beat, spun midair and accelerated to a blur back to me. He crossed the finish line under what had to be a hundred paparazzi-flashes and leaped right into my arms.

Shocked, I staggered backward, barely holding on from his considerable momentum. His slobbery lick about did me in. Yuck! I squelched my instinct to pull away. Every eye focused right on Bayle and me.

I felt a nail-biting anticipation. Waiting for what, I had no idea. Until Alan Thorpe's voice exploded over the loudspeaker.

"The new national course run time belongs to Outfoxing Pi. Bayle Fountaine is the fastest flyball dog on record."

Thunderous applause erupted as the crowd roared to their feet. The sweeping excitement even got me, until I saw Tina, her head bowed holding onto Bolt as if he were a lifeline. Howard's grand plan came together today. I guess I'm glad I'd been a part of it.

Bayle's warm body snuggled close, happily sharing his glory, safely in my arms. Suddenly, I got Rayelle's attachment to this high-maintenance dog and Howard's drive to get them both on his team. Even why someone might kill to have him.

CHAPTER 21

I didn't want to believe Tina had anything to do with her husband's murder, but that Norman Bates look she'd flashed Bayle last night still sent chills up my spine. Add her considerable motive, and I had to keep digging. I still dreaded Howard's wake. Since my father's and Aunt Char's husband's deaths, I found traditional mourning untenable.

Tina's decision to hold Howard's wake at Ciao Bella made no sense until I entered the Tuscan-inspired restaurant the following day. Gone were the elegant white-linen tablecloths and padded straight-backed chairs, replaced by cozy Old World alcoves furnished with leather couches and barrel chairs surrounding rough-hewn coffee tables that melded with the Capalbio frescos and a fifty-year photo chronicle of the Principato family's passage to Barkview by way of Ellis Island. White lilies, roses, and irises overflowed pottery urns. Except for a wicker basket filled with traditional Chinese red coin envelopes beside the guest book, I felt like an extra on *The Sopranos*.

That Tina had managed the makeover after last night's

dinner service and flyball races said a lot about her managerial skills and her family's support network. Even now, Tina's sisters-in-law and the restaurant's waitstaff filled drink orders and passed canapés to the hundred-plus guests. Although Tina's extended family accounted for half of the attendees, a who's who of Barkview residents also paid their respects.

A freshly groomed Bayle beneath my feet, Sandy and I nursed fluted Bellinis as we watched our vote-hungry mayor huddle with Barkview's dot.com land developer. The chief and Russ blended in, dressed in dark slacks and shirts. They'd staked out opposing corners, helping us complete an eagle-eyed observation triangle.

"Shame on the mayor." Dressed in dark slacks and a blouse, with her long hair knotted at her nape, Sandy looked chicly solemn.

No one had ever accused the mayor of having taste. Aunt Char had attended the church service, but chose not to attend this event. Not that I blamed her. My uncle's funeral still stuck with me, too.

"What did you find out about Alan's daughter Tiffany?" I asked.

Sandy rubbed her hands in pure delight. This ought to be good. "Well, her motocross tag is T Racer. She was at an event in San Bernardino the night of Howard's murder."

"That's only ninety minutes from here."

"She easily could've driven here and back."

"There was something off about her at the flyball race last night," I admitted.

"She could've been high. T has been in rehab for opioid addiction. Rumor has it she failed her motocross drug test," Sandy said.

"That's interesting. No reason for her to stay at the event. Is she overmedicating a bike injury?"

"Two years ago, she shattered her leg and cracked her pelvis and two discs. Spent a month in the hospital. I'd bet she's in constant pain."

Alan's overprotectiveness made perfect sense. "With Howard gone, Alan gets a nice payoff and the flyball team."

"Could be motive," Sandy agreed.

"Could be. Thank you for jumping on this."

"No problem. Are you still planning on cooking for Sunday's show?"

"Still hoping for a miracle." Me cooking for dogs had to be some cosmic joke.

I expected a Sandyism, not her wandering attention. "Uh, I'm going to mingle." She snagged a fresh Bellini from a passing tray and beelined it to the entry where she met Sean Riley, the man with more secrets than Russ.

I downed my drink in a single gulp. Much as I wanted to stop that train wreck, I had no right to dictate her personal life.

Ariana's arrival refocused my attention, and I waved her my way. Dressed in black with a starched white oxford blouse and discreet diamond studs, she looked more preppy than a successful jewelry store owner. Gem sat in regal splendor at her side, her jeweled collar twinkling in the incandescent lights.

"What did you find on the diamond I found in Bayle's tail?" I asked.

"Good to see you, too, Catalina," Ariana said. "I see you and Bayle have reached an understanding."

"Hardly. I live in constant fear of his next misadventure."

A chuckle escaped Ariana's pressed lips.

"Rethinking your catty zero tolerance comments, I see."

I hung my head. Ariana instantly sobered. "I hate these things. Remembering is not a comfort."

An avoidance subscriber myself, I recognized the signs. I

swear even Gem eyed her funny. Ariana never discussed her past. Aunt Char, who counted Ariana as a pal, knew little about her life before Barkview.

I pressed this rare moment of insight. "Closure is different for everyone."

Flanked by her mother and older brother, Tina stood at the entrance where I'd greeted her on my arrival, patting hands and accepting condolences. She seemed atypically calm.

"She's on Valium," Ariana remarked.

Seemed likely. "Or Xanax."

Ariana nodded. "I have asked around about the diamond. Nothing to report yet."

"But you're the only jeweler in town." No luck hiding my disappointment. I'd been counting on her.

Ariana bristled. "Except for Samuel's and Sons at the Old Barkview Inn."

"You're the only one that matters." A Rodeo Drive-quality jewelry store in Barkview made no sense to me. This was a dog town. Merchandise should reflect that.

Ariana's stop-hand ended further comment. "Have no fear. I have personally contacted them and shops in the surrounding area. It's possible the owner hasn't realized the diamond is missing yet."

The diamond had been small. "Any other revelations?" I smiled despite the circumstances.

"I have discovered a genuine interest in old-cut diamonds," Ariana announced.

"You're kidding."

"That cut does reduce the diamond sparkle to a lifeless blob versus the modern, multi-facetted brilliant cut that taps into a seductive fire, but there is still something haunting about it," Ariana explained.

Far be it from me to question the woman who made a healthy living catering to retail whims?

"I'd like to display Celeste Barklay's Old World diamond Cavalier collection in a mini-event to compliment the Smithsonian's Shepard Diamond exhibition for the Founder's Day celebration."

"Aunt Char will be honored to show off the Barklay collection. The promotion can't hurt her mayoral chances either." My gaze found the incumbent mayor now politicking with Barkview's sanitation czar.

"That's what friends are for." Ariana sniffed.

Aunt Char did have her fair share. Tina's exclamation drew our attention to the entry, where Stephan held a black fuzz ball.

"Ah, the newest twist." Ariana selected two champagne flutes from a passing tray. She handed one to me and took a long sip from hers.

I leaned in, prepared for a zinger. "Do tell."

"Baby Blue Bell will need to keep him warm at night."

No revelation there. There had to be more.

Ariana did not disappoint. "The night of Howard's murder. That noise..."

"The one you and Chris didn't hear?" No wonder she'd come to see me and avoided the chief. Although people often recalled pertinent details after a crime, Ariana's furtive glance said she just decided to share.

"Honestly, I didn't think it was anything, but..."

This was a big "but."

"The more I think about it, the more I think I heard a Vespa."

"The Vespa Guardian?" Despite my best effort, skepticism laced my tone.

Her gaze narrowed. "Ghosts, Catalina?"

I felt like an idiot. "Sorry."

"The whole idea of Stephan's VW making the backfiring noise did not make sense. Why would he drive a noisy, recognizable car two blocks to kill Howard?"

My argument too. I played the video I'd taken of Tiffany Thorpe's Honda motorcycle. "Listen to this. Could that be the noise you heard?"

Ariana's drawn brows gave no hint. Finally, she said, "Play it again."

I did. Afraid to hope.

She stroked her chin. "I'm sorry. I cannot swear to it."

Ugh! So much for exonerating Rayelle. Me leading Sunday's cooking show loomed.

Ariana had more to show me. She beckoned me to the nearest alcove and pointed out an old photo. I leaned in to be sure. A much younger Nonna smiled ear-to-ear astride a vintage black Vespa.

"Thirty years ago Tina's grandmother drove that thing like an Indy 500 racer. My first day in Barkview, she nearly ran me over on First Street."

"That big sycamore is a blind spot." Who hadn't had a heart-pumping encounter there?

"That tree was barely a sapling back then and I was standing on the sidewalk," Ariana insisted.

Appropriate or not, my chuckle drew notice from everyone within earshot. Ariana continued undeterred. "Tina's mother got the gene, too. The boys"—She pointed to Tina's uncles scattered across the room—"souped up the engine. That scooter moved." Ariana scrolled on her phone, finally playing a Vespa engine YouTube video. "That is not exactly what I heard, but close."

Excitement bubbled up in me. Could the *rat-ta-ta* and

voorum sounds have been a Vespa with a modified engine? "Why haven't I ever seen it?"

"I never saw it again after Tina's mom got a speeding ticket on it."

"Seriously? Was she in a school zone?"

"Hardly. Cops clocked me at sixty on First Street." Dressed entirely in black with her hair in a loose chignon, Tina's mother, Angela, looked more ethereal than somber in a matronly kind of way. "Worse, I didn't make curfew either. I was grounded for a month." She hugged Ariana. "Dad was a real…" She bit her lower lip.

"Something, all right," Ariana said.

"That he was," Angela agreed. "I shudder to think about Tina ever driving that vehicle."

Although Tina's grandfather had passed before I arrived in Barkview, his legendary ornery personality lived on. "What happened to the Vespa?" I asked, maybe too eagerly.

Angela stiffened. "Dad sold it back in 1985." She motioned to her butt. "My rear end still smarts. Mama didn't talk to him or me for the whole miserable month I was grounded. The house was a war zone. Dad said he tried to buy it back, but the Vespa had been scrapped for parts. He gave Mama the tailpipe as a peace offering."

Tina's uncle, a male version of her mom, came out of nowhere. "Dad really tried. He gave her the rearview mirror for Christmas that year and a clutch for her birthday."

Angela's clenched jaw begged for an argument. "Some things you just can't recover from."

"Mama wasn't reasonable," Tina's brother explained. "He bought her Vespa parts for every birthday, anniversary, and Christmas until he died."

Angela's cough barely covered a curse. "In the end, it made great fodder for the Vespa Guardian myth."

I knew it. "You started the legend?"

Angela's lopsided grin confirmed it. "If my kids ever ask, I'll deny it. I did it to protect my daughter from making the same mistakes I did."

"And singlehandedly kept an entire generation in line," Ariana commented. "Hard to believe you all survived youth."

Mystery solved. No wonder no one knew the Vespa Guardian's origins. If the whole thing was made up, what had Gabby and Stephanie seen? Could there be someone out there bringing this so-called ghost to life? I won't put it past Angela to perpetuate the myth, considering her miserable marriage. "Did Nonna reassemble the Vespa?" All eyes questioned my sanity.

Angela patted my arm. "You don't just reassemble a vehicle like that. I bet the parts are still around here somewhere, though. Mama's a hoarder."

Angela's brother added, "I remember moving three boxes when she moved back here."

"I'm shocked she didn't dump them over his grave," Angela remarked.

"Mama would never..." Tina's uncle's shock seemed genuine.

Nonna's plate-launching temper indicated otherwise. Stubbornness aside, how did one hide a Vespa in a small town? The real question was, did she or anyone else actually have one? Since YouTube videos replicated the Vespa sound perfectly, any quiet vehicle with a blaring audio cellphone could create the illusion.

Angela's shrill phone alarm interrupted further discussion. "Nonna's upstairs. I'm, uh, the closest. Excuse me. Joey needs me." After a quick wave across the room to Tina, Angela pivoted and marched through the swinging kitchen door.

Tina's brother bid us farewell and escaped, leaving Ariana and me.

"Was it something I said?" Ariana asked tongue in cheek.

After being around Joey, I had a pretty good idea what was happening. From their respective corners, I noted Russ and Uncle G sharing a knowing look.

Ariana shook her head. "Undoubtedly, none of our business."

I had the good sense to blush. "I am a reporter. Secrets make me crazy."

"You're an executive producer now." Her reminder stung. "Curiosity killed the cat, you know."

I sputtered peach-infused Prosecco. Trust Ariana to hold nothing back. "I'm still a reporter deep down. I-I can't help myself."

"Russ is a good man," Ariana said meaningfully. "Remember that."

My gaze sought Russ. Cornered by Gabby beside the fountain, he might well be a candidate for sainthood, given the way he patiently listened to her monologue. Why did not knowing his secrets make me so crazy? Why couldn't I just let it go? I knew he'd protect me and Aunt Char. Was that enough?

Part of me even wanted it to be. The other part... Ariana retreated before I could rebut, making me feel like the cad left on the dance floor.

Maybe I was. Since walking away wasn't an option, confirming that the infamous Vespa parts remained unassembled topped my to-do list. According to Angela's brother, the garage/receiving area adjacent to the kitchen promised to be the best place to start.

Getting in the kitchen posed a problem. Simply entering just seemed bold. Bayle's it's-time-to-chase-ball bark offered a chance. I rummaged through my shoulder bag finally locating the ball I'd finally remembered to pack. I shook it to get his attention, waited for a server to exit, and then launched it through the opening. Bayle, being Bayle, gave chase, his leash clanking on the terra-cotta floor in hot pursuit. I followed, half-heartedly demanding he heel.

I stumbled over Bayle seated smack in the middle of the doorway into the stainless steel commercial kitchen. From the gigantic hooded range-top and igloo-shaped pizza oven to the center prep station table overhung by pots, pans, and dried oregano, basil, and rosemary bunches, the space reminded me of my grandma's kitchen. Joey sat at the prep counter, his head in his hands on the countertop and his feet dangling from the stool. Angela stroked his shoulder while Bolt nudged his leg.

"Are you okay?" I asked.

Joey's glazed-over eyes scared me. Did he even recognize me?

"It's nothing. His blood sugar is low." No reaction from Joey despite Angela's brusqueness. "Finish the juice."

It had to be more. The boy's olive complexion looked ghostly.

Angela read my concern. "It's just too much stress for him." Her frown deepened as she glanced at her phone. "Pronto, Joey. Drink the juice. We have guests waiting."

Joey sipped the drink. "I'm 'kay, Nana." I hardly recognized Joey's squeaky voice.

He wasn't okay, and his grandmother vulture-hovering wasn't helping any. "I-I'll stay with him." How hard could it be? With Bolt and Bayle flanking Joey, he wasn't going anywhere.

Angela's frown lines lessened. She tapped something on her phone. "His blood sugar is rising."

Numbers flashed on the screen. 89, 90... "Is that how you track it?"

"Yes. It's much easier than pricking his finger for a blood test."

Ouch. I sympathy-rubbed my index fingertip. "I understand." I did. Of course the people who cared for Joey would have the same tracking system, including Howard. Suddenly, realization struck. Anyone monitoring Joey's app had known Howard's location the night he was murdered.

I noted Angela's furtive look toward the exit. Guilt? I wasn't sure. "Wow! This kitchen is huge. It must take hours to clean up every night."

"An hour or so. Tina and I make a good team." Angela tapped her phone and scrolled through the data again. The blinking red numbers held at 90.

"So, what happened Sunday night?" I asked.

"We made limoncello."

"Yum." My timely response drew Angela's half-smile.

"My cousin from Italy called, too. Tina played her relaxation music so loud, I had to go into the dining room to hear."

"You told the chief you were together in the kitchen." Was this a break in their alibi? I tempered my enthusiasm as Angela's sharp look challenged my composure.

"Tina did not leave the kitchen. I was right outside."

With plates and knives within easy reach, I chose agreeability. That the Ciao Bella perimeter alarm had not been disarmed during that time confirmed her statement. The nuance bothered me, though. "How long were you on the phone with your cousin?"

"Thirty minutes or an hour."

More likely an hour, the way Angela talked. Plenty of time for Tina to walk to Bichon Bisquets, kill Howard and return. But how had she exited the building?

Relief lightened Angela's expression. "Joey's blood sugar is back to normal. Make sure he finishes his juice." More softly, she continued, "Thank you for staying with him. My daughter needs me. She's not as strong as she lets on." With mother-bear intent, Angela disappeared through the swinging door.

Tina not a pillar of strength? Hard to believe.

I ruffled Joey's hair. "You okay?"

His glassy gaze met mine. "Yeah. I shouldn't have given Bolt my breakfast."

No kidding. "Why did you?"

His cheeks flushed crimson. "No one cares about Dad. They"—His Tina-like gesture included the whole world—"only care what everyone else thinks."

Tina's close-knit family? "Well. There's a lot of people out there who liked and admired your dad. I did." I spoke the truth. Odd as I found him to be, Howard's many accomplishments could not be denied.

Joey sniffed. "I guess."

Bayle nudged my calf, nearly pushing me into Joey. I got the message and hugged Joey tight. "You know, I lost my dad when I was twelve. It stinks."

Sudden tears glistened in his chocolate-brown eyes. "Do you miss him?"

"Every day."

"What if I forget?"

"You won't. Ever. I promise. Just remember the anagram game."

A smile almost cracked through his pressed lips. His arms squeezed my waist.

Russ caught us mid-hug. "You after my girl, young man?"

Joey jerked back and stuffed his hands in his pockets. "No-no, sir."

"Good." Russ snatched a thin breadstick from the table jar and brandished it like a sword. "En garde."

Russ's playfulness warmed me and should've prompted

Joey's smile, maybe even a chuckle. Not an open-mouthed gape. Childhood was all about frivolity. Surely, Howard had played with his son.

Caught up in the repartee, I swiped another breadstick, prepared to fight. "I shall defend myself conquering knight." My breadstick connected with Russ's and broke off the tip.

"You endeavor to unman me, madam?"

Guilt shot a million possibilities through my mind. I had to be beet-red. He couldn't possibly know I'd been looking into Howard's device. Or could he? The man read me way too well.

Fortunately, Bolt wiggled between us, effectively squelching the mock battle and any halfhearted denial. When Bolt licked Russ's hand, Joey relaxed.

"You two coming back outside?" Russ asked.

"Joey's helping me find something." I gestured toward the garage exit.

Russ huddled in. "Can I help?"

"You bet. We're looking for a Vespa."

Russ peeked under the table. "In the kitchen?"

"No, silly." Joey wiped his nose on his sleeve. "In the garage. Nonna told me I could drive hers when I'm old enough."

I shared a glance with Russ. Was the Vespa real after all? "A Vespa hunt it is then," Russ conceded. "Lead the way."

Joey rabbit-darted to the door. Amazing what proper blood sugar levels did both physically and emotionally. Bayle and Bolt refused to be left behind. They followed Joey into a maze of stacked tables and padded, straight-backed chairs crammed in a surefire code violation. I envied Bayle his size as he scooted between table legs while Russ and I wished for knee protection. Russ quit after toppling the first chair wall and returned to watch from the doorway.

I persisted, trying hard not to think about my dry cleaning

bill as I ducked and crawled beneath tables. I caught up with Joey a few minutes later in front of a storage rack on the back wall with three dusty-blue tarps.

Lottery fever took over. Sizewise, any of the three could be covering a Vespa. I ripped off the nearest tarp. The big reveal fell flat. What the...? Even a good look at the stainless steel contraption offered no identity clue. I sneezed.

"It's a sausage caser." Chest puffed and standing what had to be two inches taller, Joey looked like a ruling monarch. "It works..."

I tuned his Howard-worthy explanation out. Flavorful grilled sausages were a summer go-to in my house. No sense jeopardizing that.

"This is"—Joey lifted another tarp—"the pasta die my Poppa brought from Italy. It makes the best fresh pasta."

Flying dust practically blinded me as I looked at a surprisingly tarnish-free copper showerhead mounted on a medieval steel contraption.

"Did your mother tell you about the machine?" Joey's pride and enthusiasm reflected Tina's when she spoke about the restaurant.

"Mom works all the time. Nonna showed me the old pictures. I'm tall like her brother Vito." Joey stood even straighter. "I'm already taller than she is."

Hardly noteworthy. "What does your mother say about the machines?"

"That I don't need to know about them because Bianca will run the restaurant. I will be a doctor. My father said I could be a doctor after I go to Caltech like he did."

Talk about old-school sexism. "How do you feel about that?" Why was I talking about the future with a nine-year-old?

"I like to cook. Nonna taught me to make sauce. She says I make it better than Vito and he cooked at the Vati... in Rome."

"At the Vatican?"

Joey nodded. "He's a priest."

Tina had a Vatican priest in her family? Who knew?

Daunting as the obstacle course separating me from the remaining tarp appeared, my curiosity drove me. My abused shins piled on complaints as I lifted the last tarp.

Two double-stacked, oil-stained boxes sagged in the dim light. Joey opened the top box and removed a rearview mirror. No way did this pile of junk amount to an operational Vespa. I exhaled in relief. Deep down, I hadn't wanted Tina to be involved.

That left Alan Thorpe's daughter's Honda as my only possible vehicle. Although Sandy had uncovered a flaw in her alibi, that crazy theory wasn't going to clear Rayelle.

My bruised shins rejected a return trip through the furniture maze, so I maneuvered toward the rolling door. Joey scampered ahead of me, with Bayle and Bolt nosing for position at his heels. Over his shoulder he called, "Last one there is a rotten egg." Gotta love the kid's dexterity.

Me, leave a challenge unanswered? I lurched forward, disturbing a chair pile as I cleared the last table. I would've overtaken him except Bayle tangled between my legs and my feet skidded out from beneath me, sending me sprawling. I fell backward in an exaggerated slow motion that I swear Hollywood could make millions using. I landed flat on my back on the concrete, my purse smack up against the rolling door.

My scream drewRuss's concern. "Where are you? Are you all right?"

"I'm okay. Just tripped over Bayle." I envisioned Russ shoving the furniture aside with a caber-tossing Scotsman's fervor. I rolled to my right side and took inventory. Ankle, knee, elbow, wrist all seemed to work. Bayle pounced on my chest, puppy-wiggling and licking my face.

Yuck! I sputtered, turned my head right and then left, anything to escape, but that tongue just kept coming. I finally hugged him tight, smothering the wiggling. Problem solved. Until the dog squirmed free, leaving a cotton-candy-pink pawprint trail right down the front of my silk blouse. Of course, it wasn't anything I could just brush off either, but an oily mystery gunk I doubted even my laundry wizard could remove.

It was, I realized suddenly, the same gunk that Bayle had stepped in outside Bichon Bisquets the night of Howard's murder.

CHAPTER 22

A guy sniffing my blouse front with bloodhound intensity should've creeped me out. Russ identifying the muck as a clue made it all right.

"Coolant?" We'd huddled away from prying eyes in Ciao Bella's babbling fountain courtyard. Bayle cuddled beside me on the Romanesque bench facing the classical three-tier fountain, mesmerized by the frolicking bird-bathers. To be a dog...

"Antifreeze. Yes. Even in California." Amusement laced Russ's tone. "Don't let the full maintenance package on your car lapse."

Excellent advice. A car expert I was not.

"Your blouse isn't a total loss," he continued. "A quick spot clean with dish soap and a soft-bristle toothbrush should clean it. If that doesn't work, a baking soda paste..."

If not for the cool offshore breeze, I'd have handed him the blouse right then and there. Just add laundry guru to his ever-expanding list of keep-this-guy points.

"You found dusty boxed parts, but no Vespa." He crouched

to Bayle's eye-level. "The question is, how did you get coolant on your paws, my man?"

Bayle barked twice and rolled onto his back, lapping up the paw scrub and belly scratch.

Talk about envy. "Me next," I blurted. Who wouldn't crave Russ's expert touch?

"That can be arranged...later." His suggestive grin brought to mind too many blush-inducing images.

My pout got me nowhere. Of course, a dog tracking muck everywhere came first. "I swear I should change Bayle's name to Velcro. Everything sticks to him."

"That it does. Which begs the question..."

I really hated Russ's "You're busted" pauses. I gulped.

"How exactly did Bayle walk on your chest?"

Caught again. "Well, Joey stopped right in front of me, and I tripped over Bayle and..." Maybe racing Joey through the furniture maze had been reckless. How did Russ always catch my misdeeds?

"Who promptly walked all over you?" There was no censure in his voice, yet I felt reprimanded.

"Next time, win."

I flushed. Redirecting seemed a better plan than denial. "The interesting part is I think this"—I pointed to the cotton-candy pink on Bayle's paws—"is the same stuff Rayelle washed off Bayle's paws the night Howard was killed."

He stiffened, suddenly all business. "Is the stain on anything else?"

I nodded. Circumventing his all-knowingness felt good. "My jeans..."

"Tell me you haven't washed them."

"Not before the hamper overflows."

His smile broadened.

"A point for procrastination," I suggested.

No comment, just his brow arched in acknowledgment. "Tell me you know where Bayle stepped in the coolant."

"Had to be by the plant at Bichon Bisquets' entrance."

Russ put Bayle on the ground. He looked from Russ to his sticks-for-feet and barked.

I laughed. Couldn't help myself. "You need a Fluff and Buff refresher."

Russ joined in. "Sorry, buddy." Bayle huffed, but followed us to Russ's Land Rover. He opened the door for Bayle and me.

The dog jumped into my lap and neck-nudged me as Russ bagged the cleaning rag. I knew I should've objected because by the time we'd turned onto Maple, Bayle's damp feet had soaked through my slacks.

"Do I want to know what you were doing hiding behind the plant?" Russ asked as he drove north on First Street.

"I never said we were hiding. We weren't spying on the chief, either, if that's what you're thinking. We'd just seen Howard..." My voice cracked.

"I'm sorry." He meant it too.

"What does the coolant really prove? I didn't find the Vespa. Or any evidence one exists."

"Not yet. We may be able to establish a link between the locations. We might also be able to narrow the vehicle search based on the type of coolant and composition," Russ suggested.

"And exonerate Rayelle?" Bayle's head popped off my lap at her name. I scratched his head.

"It's a long shot."

"We have nothing else." My frustration just seeped out. "It's been four days..."

"Patience, Cat. Breakthroughs sometimes come from unexpected sources."

I heard his words, even believed him, but his friend wasn't in prison. "Not helping."

His hand covered mine. "Sometimes you just have to move on."

I frowned. I wasn't ready to give up on Rayelle yet.

Russ hung a U-turn and parked right in front of Bichon Bisquets. Although the police perimeter tape had been removed, an oversized neon CLOSED sign dominated the darkened bay window. The empty café tables just needed a tumbleweed blowing by to depict a ghost-worthy town. Even the neighboring businesses seemed deserted.

Bayle agreed. After one long, sky-pointed sniff, he refused to exit until Russ lifted him off my lap. Once outside, the dog hugged my legs.

Russ removed a black evidence collection case and digital camera from his Land Rover and followed me to the purple lilac urn.

"Rayelle and I were here." I pointed to the three-foot space between the building and urn. Sure enough, a small pinkish watermark stained the concrete. Scratch my theory that an electric scooter with a recording had mimicked the Vespa sound. A vehicle had parked here.

Russ snapped pictures in rapid succession. "The amount of coolant indicates the vehicle did stay here long." He scraped the residue with a knife blade and flaked it into a vial.

I tempered my enthusiasm as I looked up and down the block. "This makes no sense. Why would a murderer hide a getaway vehicle here? You can clearly see it from the street."

I followed Russ' eagle eye around the perimeter. "At midnight in Barkview?"

Point made since no direct light shone on the area. Rayelle and I had taken refuge here because of the long shadows... because of what we'd seen. I sucked in my breath, remembering the metallic smell, the ghostly cast to Howard's skin, the knife sticking out of his back. No one deserved to die that way. The guilty person had to pay.

"I'm not buying your theory that Howard's murder was a crime of opportunity," I announced too loudly.

No confirmation or denial. Russ just methodically labeled the evidence.

Enough of his fence-sitting secrecy. The person meeting Howard the night of his murder knew his location in advance. So did Tina. If I shared my evidence, would he? "Tina knew Howard was here."

I squirmed under Russ's long look. "Her alibi is solid. She is on camera inside the restaurant and no one exited the building during the murder window."

"Could her security camera times have been changed?" A very TV concept I knew, but...

"No," Russ said simply.

"Did Tina call anyone?" Stephan, maybe.

"No. Tina's mother received an incoming call. She was on the phone for fifty-seven minutes at the restaurant."

I breathed easier. I'd done my part. We'd come full circle. "Who was Howard meeting, Russ?" I'd played by his rules long enough. I needed to know.

Russ knew. I saw the confirmation in his piercing glaze. His refusal to share hurt. Rayelle hadn't murdered Howard. Russ knew it. And he knew I knew it. "Rayelle doesn't belong in jail," I announced.

"She's safer there," Russ said.

Uncle G had said the same thing. "If you think that's an answer, you are wrong," I snapped.

"It's going to have to be for now." Russ's expression remained unchanged.

I should've just stamped my feet. Instead, I blurted out, "Who is Marcos Ramirez Hernandez II?"

Forget plausible deniability. I'd gone too far. I'd dug exactly where he'd specifically asked me not to. Anger, disappointment, and something that looked a lot like concern played across his suddenly shadowed features. "Cat, hear me. You need to leave this alone."

As if I could. I started to come out swinging, but his unwavering tone acted like an ice bath down my spine. "This is no armchair puzzle for you to solve. Your life, your Aunt Char's life, Sandy's life... Anyone you care about you put at risk going down that path."

He'd sucker punched me. I'd do anything to protect my aunt and Sandy and... "W-what about you?"

His gaze held mine as he took my hand in his. "I am humbled by your concern, but this is what I do, Cat. It's not glamorous. It's not always safe and there are no guarantees."

Losing him wasn't an option. I blinked away tears. He pulled me into his embrace. "Until I met you, I had no weaknesses. Now..." He kissed my hair. "If anything happened to you... You are going to have to trust that I can take care of myself. I can't be worrying about you."

I sucked in my breath. Marcos had to be a really bad guy. I did trust Russ. His forefinger tipped my chin upward and his lips hovered over mine, promising...

"Your word you will not dig into Marcos Ramirez Hernandez II. I need to know. I must know you are safe."

I wanted to fight on. I really did, but... I nodded. "Is he why Howard left Tina and the kids?" I didn't need to define "he"; the evil specter stood between us.

"All I will say is Howard was a good man who died protecting his family."

Now that I believed. "Why do you still have Rayelle in custody?"

"There is a small chance she may be a target."

"Because Bichon Bisquets was a drop?" His arms stiffened around me. "Omg. The old gallery was the drop. Rayelle was just in the wrong place. Howard put her at risk."

His forefinger pressed against my lips. I'd nailed it all right.

"My gut is still telling me someone close to Howard killed him," Russ said.

I wanted to argue with his remarkably reliable intuition. "Because the Bichon knife in his back wasn't a professional hit?" No details needed. Hollywood's many gangster versions worked just fine for me.

"It still had to have been planned," I continued. "Wearing metallic clothing. Staging the getaway vehicle. No way the killer just happened to see Howard sitting alone in Bichon Bisquets and popped in to kill him."

"The Bichon knife indicates spontaneity."

"Or a frame."

"Rayelle is new to town. Who would want to frame her?"

Good question. As if the pranks alone weren't enough. Harmless as they were, could they have just been a starting point? I took a step back, a sudden chill separating us. "I need to find the leaky coolant getaway vehicle."

"That's a start. Come on. Let's look around for more coolant."

"A breadcrumb trail?"

"Yes, ma'am." That sexy twinkle in his eye resonated. Different as we were, we shared that high for the hunt.

We circled the building twice without luck. It wasn't until Bayle detoured to where we'd found Howard's parked car. Crazy as it sounded, he sniffed around the area, sat right next to a faint, almost indiscernible pink droplet, and whined.

How could he possibly have known that was what we were looking for? The dog couldn't read my mind. Or could he?

Russ questioned nothing. He simply praised Bayle with a butt scratch and recorded the evidence. I speculated, "The vehicle had to have been in Ciao Bella's garage for some time, based on how much you cleaned off Bayle's feet."

Russ's shrug neither confirmed nor denied that theory.

"What's bothering me is, why would the perpetrator stop at Howard's car after killing him?" I asked.

"Could've been before the murder," Russ suggested.

Good point. If the killer was familiar with Bolt, he'd assume Howard was nearby. Talking through a problem always helped me find perspective. I appreciated Russ's insight.

"Bolt likely knew the killer, based on the reports of him barking."

"That's not helpful. Bolt is a popular guy around town. He knows just about everyone." I chewed my lower lip. "I know Alan's daughter Tiffany was at a motocross event during Howard's murder, but Ariana thinks her Honda 125 might be the sound she heard."

"Might be?"

"I know it's not prosecutable, but Tiffany's Honda was parked next to Alan's car at flyball practice last night. If there's a coolant leak..."

We moved together toward his Land Rover. Finding coolant at the flyball parking lot would be a start. I still needed to place her at the crime scene and tie her to Ciao Bella.

"Why do you suspect her?"

"There was something off about her last night. Alan and Howard also disagreed about the direction of the team."

No need to explain which team. "Enough to kill?"

"I don't know. Alan has full control of the team now and did benefit financially. I know. I'm reaching for straws."

Tina working with Tiffany just didn't compute either.

CHAPTER 23

Connecting Tiffany didn't work out as I'd hoped. Barkview's ever-efficient city maintenance had emptied every trash can, sanitized the restrooms and washed down the concrete before our arrival.

Time to track down her motorcycle.

I declined Russ's offer for a ride back to my car, instead walking Bayle the few blocks to the Graveyards and Ghosts office. The pee-on-every-tree-fest took twice as long as I expected, and I arrived both overheated and exasperated.

Not the best attitude for a fact-finding mission. I took a few calming breaths before following the gravestone path past the Frosty Pups Creamery and into the alley. The open roll-up garage door invited an overview of the property in a single glance. Sure enough, ten fat-tire scooters lined the right side of the lobby while Stephan, dressed in the familiar Old West undertaker's outfit, leaned on a bar-height counter.

"What's happenin'?" He flipped me the surfer's baby-finger–thumb shake. Dark sunglasses hid his real reaction.

I approached, noting the bluish-black fluff-ball at his feet. "The phantom Vespa is leaking coolant."

He lifted his glasses, his piercing blue gaze meeting mine. "And you just figured my Bug would be worth checking out?"

Hardly the laid-back surfer dude here. "Nope. Electric scooters wouldn't be candidates, either, unless you had a Vespa recording."

I expected a chuckle, maybe even a shrug. Not an eye-opening aha moment. Surely he didn't really believe in ghosts? I went in another direction. "I figured you see the beach crowd daily. Anyone with a suspect vehicle?"

Stephan scratched his chin, his laissez-faire persona back in place. "Most folks travel on skateboards or razor scooters. Did you check out the OBI?"

"Not yet. The Old Barkview Inn only rents beach bikes and Segways." Neither would leak coolant. I was getting nowhere fast. With no surveillance cameras in or around the Frosty Pups Creamery, I had no choice but to believe Stephanie's alibi for her brother or try to find collaborating guests.

Stephan knew exactly where I was going. "Two tubas closed us down Sunday night. Barkview High beat San Diego at their band competition."

They should be easy enough to find. "Those boys happen to be surfers, too?"

"They're girls. One likes strawberry yogurt with piles of gummy bears and the other mocha with nuts."

Impressive order recall. The Stephan enigma continued.

"I didn't like Howard Looc," he announced. "That's no secret, but I didn't kill him either."

I believed him. Despite his feelings for Tina, he hadn't been conspiring with her either. My suspect pool kept shrinking. What was I missing?

Suddenly, a blue-black fluff barreled around the counter and skidded into Bayle. Puffy white careened with fluffy black and piled into a scooter tire. Bayle's single *Yikes!* bark drew my giggle.

Stephan moved like the Flash around the counter. Too late. The line of fat-tire scooters fell like dominoes. Bayle's paws covered his ears. No remorse from Triple B. She squatted and peed beside the nearest tire until Stephan grasped the puppy by the scruff and hauled her outside. "Puppy training."

Ugh. I watched the yellowish puddle creep toward my feet. Bayle, no doubt hoping for a reprimand-free retreat, pulled me toward the door. Escape the better part of valor, I headed south on the boardwalk. Stephan acknowledged my farewell without a break in his one-sided discussion with Triple B on a grassy patch. Potty training by lecture? Call me skeptical regarding that tactic.

I called Sandy while half-walking, half-dragging Bayle along First Street. I drew the line at one daily sniff-a-thon. Time to retrieve my car.

Sandy answered on the first ring. "I'm sorry, Boss, but I have nothing on Marcos…"

Probably the best news I'd heard all day. "Stop everything on him. No internet searches. No electronic signature. Nothing."

"Russ's request?" she asked, almost too softly.

"More like order. He must be a pretty bad guy." I didn't even want to repeat his name.

"Got it. Request wiped."

"Can you find out what time the two tubas from Barkview's marching band saw Stephan Sunday night?"

"You don't think Stephan did it, do you?" Sandy asked.

"I doubt it. I did discover that Tina and her mom were not in the same room during Howard's murder."

Sandy's long pause stirred up my doubts. "So, Tina and her

mother were in the same building and the perimeter alarm remained unbroken?"

"Russ told me Tina's mom was on the phone with her cousin in Italy for about an hour."

"That's enough time for Tina to murder Howard and return, but how did she know where Howard was?" Sandy asked.

Even after I explained the bare-bones technology regarding Joey's tracker, either of them murdering Howard sounded pretty unlikely.

"I need to find any vehicle with a coolant leak right now."

"Our ghost is having mechanical issues?"

"With any luck." We were sure due some.

"W-e-l-l. We may just have caught a break. Gabby saw Tiffany's bike at the Barkage Garage yesterday afternoon."

Good idea. Jimmy "The Engine Hummer" Daniels diagnosed engine issues like a true master. He'd know if Tiffany's Honda had coolant issues.

"I'll also check the vehicles registered in Barkview for something that sounds like a Vespa," Sandy said.

"Stephan suggested I visit the Old Barkview Inn."

"Don't they just rent Segways and beach bikes?" Sandy asked.

"That's what I thought. They may have a few golf carts for the maintenance crew and who knows what else in their garage. The thing that bothers me is maybe I'm not looking for a Vespa. What if someone is playing a Vespa recording while driving another vehicle?"

"That's pretty devious. It would have to be a quiet vehicle like an electric scooter," Sandy suggested. "The vehicle of choice for the Graveyards and Ghosts tours."

True, but the theory had created a raw, disbelieving reaction from Stephan. "I don't think Stephan is doing this." I sucked in my breath. "Turns out, Angela Principato created the Vespa Guardian."

Sandy's hoot tickled my funny bone. "Shut up."

"She oh-so-proudly admitted it, too."

"Now, I could see her driving around freaking out teenagers," Sandy said.

Me, too. "Murdering Howard, though?"

"What about that Italian revenge thing? I mean, she's short enough to be the blob, but maybe a little too round."

Rotund might be a more accurate word. "Before we get all Hollywood Mafia, how did she get out of the building with the alarm on?"

Sandy's long exhale never boded well. "You're right. I just wanted a suspect. Any suspect besides Rayelle."

I didn't need a PhD to see a problem here. "What happened?"

"The US Attorney's Office took over the case as part of an ongoing investigation."

I froze, Bayle's leash snapping as he jerked to an abrupt halt. He shook his head and blinked at me. I couldn't meet his stare. "No bail?"

Another long exhale. My heart sank. "No. Apparently, they can keep her indefinitely."

"Is she still in Barkview?" Real fear set in. Although Russ had warned me, I still couldn't believe it.

"According to Mark, she'll be remanded to federal custody in the morning."

I had twelve hours. Talk about motivation. I needed to solve this murder, and fast. "Find out where Tiffany parks her motorcycle. I'm heading to Jimmy's now."

CHAPTER 24

I jogged the last few blocks to my car and loaded Bayle in. Located on the corner of Seventh and Elder since 1950-something, the Barkage Garage had changed ownership in the 1980s and again in 2010. Each owner had updated the property to be able to service more advanced auto technology, but had retained the fire-engine-red gas pumps and malts-and-burgers style uniforms. Jimmy Daniels and JD Junkyard, Jimmy's scruffy part–Pit Bull, part–anyone's guess fifty-pound rescue, met me in the driveway. I rolled down my window.

"Sandy tells me you need a coolant leak." Was that promise in his orthodontically perfect smile and dancing hazel eyes? Prematurely bald, Jimmy wore a vintage Barkview Barks baseball cap.

"I do. Have any?"

He gestured for me to park alongside his black F-150 truck. Although tall by most standards, how Jimmy climbed into the tricked-out cab still puzzled me. Hope squelched my fear that JD might object and I exited the car. I did carry Bayle, unwilling to take any chances. JD stuck his broad black nose right in my crotch. Ugh. I jumped back. Couldn't help myself.

"JD." Jimmy pointed to a dog bed inside the garage bay. JD dipped his tan-spotted head and retreated. "Sorry, Cat. I'm still working on JD's manners."

"No problem." I rubbed my neck, feeling the bite scars beneath my scarf. Once upon a time I would've screamed murder. Today my blood pressure only spiked. "I'm making progress, Jimmy."

Jimmy's smile returned. "That's what I call good news. Come into my office. I pulled up every coolant leak I've worked on for the past six months."

Wow! What more could I ask for? "Thank you."

"I feel for Rayelle. Barkview's rough on newcomers."

His experienced tone bothered me. After ten years, Jimmy hardly qualified as a newbie. Aunt Char had called it. This town needed a dedicated welcome committee. She'd fix that as mayor.

Jimmy sanitized his hands and attacked his keyboard like a data retrieval pro. A minute later his printer went to work.

"Sandy said you were specifically looking for a motorcycle or scooter," Jimmy said.

I nodded, scanning the list he handed to me. "You added coolant to Ciao Bella's delivery van last week?"

"Yeah. Tina was dropping something off at the hospital and drove in for me to add it. I took a quick look. Didn't see a leak, but they can be deceptive."

"Does coolant just dissipate?"

Jimmy shrugged. "The van is ten years old. Could be a cracked hose or a tiny hole in the radiator. She said she'd bring it back for a full checkup."

A minor leak might explain coolant in Ciao Bella's garage,

but not behind the planter. "I don't see Tiffany Thorpe's motorcycle on the list."

"No issue with a coolant leak on her bike. I replaced a faulty interlock switch yesterday."

Real fear set in. I was out of suspects. Now what? "If I had a coolant sample, could you tell me what vehicle it came from?"

"Best I can tell you is the coolant brand." He stroked his salt-and-pepper stubble. "Your leak could've been fixed anywhere. Another way to tell is to look for a chalky residue on the ground strap and center spark plug electrode."

Jimmy handed me a silver-and-white thingamabob. "A spark plug?"

"I'll make a car aficionado out of you yet."

"Careful, someday I may even figure out how to gas up my car," I threatened. I took a picture of it, anyway. I'd take hope from just about anywhere now.

"And put me out of a job."

He did have my number. "Any other likely candidates?"

"No. I'll keep my eyes open."

"What's your take on the Vespa Guardian?"

His strangled laugh said far more than he'd intended. Had I stumbled onto some Barkview cultish secret? "For the record, I'm a staunch supporter."

As any father raising a high school–age cheerleader would be. "Where can I find the whole story?"

"Barkview High's bathroom walls."

I deserved that. I leaned in and whispered, "Look. Off the record. Who is the Vespa Guardian?" Okay. It sounded crazy, but his arched brow dared me to take a deeper dive. "Don't tell me the fathers take turns? You all get a weekend?" Not even a flinch. "Come on, Jimmy. I need to find the vehicle for Rayelle."

I thought I'd lost as his pause stretched. He wanted to tell me, but something checked his tongue. I didn't sense fear.

A customer drove up to the gas pump, offering escape. Over his shoulder, Jimmy said, "Try the Old Barkview Inn."

My "why?" went unanswered. I'd gotten more than I'd expected. Which wasn't much, but desperation called for drastic measures, and two suggestions to visit the same place, half-hearted as they'd been, demanded investigation.

I packed Bayle into the Jag and headed west on Elder, shading my eyes against the afternoon glare. I turned right on First Street and drove under the Victorian portico into the Old Barkview Inn's valet parking lane. The sky-blue building, accented by white gingerbread trim, had twin peaks surrounded by a widow's walk peeking out over a slate-blue gabled roof. Since 1890 it had hosted numerous Hollywood productions and heads of state from around the globe.

Bayle must've sensed my eagerness because he leaped out the passenger door as soon as the valet opened it. I lunged for the leash, but catching a wind sock couldn't be more elusive. Ugh. Purse thrashing against my hip, I sprinted after the trailing leash as it bounced across the marble entry. The mischief he could cause inside the lobby, known for elaborately hand-carved mahogany ceilings and stained-glass masterpieces, scared me.

In one practiced move, Franklin Duncan, concierge extraordinaire, scooped Bayle into his arms mere steps before he piled into a display of elaborately carved pumpkins arranged on sparkling gossamer webbing. Dressed in a gray-striped Victorian waistcoat and gentleman's ascot, he had nary a hair out of place.

My sigh of relief mixed with a collective gasp from the milling crowd admiring the historic Barkview scenes carved into fancy orange, white, light-blue, and green pumpkins and gourds. The dirty control-your-dog looks haunted me now. Sure, Bayle needed to be publicly reprimanded, but his contrite head tilt and drooping pout got right to me. He felt worse than I did.

I inhaled the normally comforting smell of beeswax and fine wood to no avail. Somehow I needed to control Bayle's exuberance. I wasn't a thoughtless, indulgent dog sitter.

Undaunted, Franklin double-looped Bayle's leash around my wrist. "Miss Wright, how can I be of service today?"

In a minute he made it all right. Little wonder he'd earned the nickname "Magician." Franklin took customer service to a level five-star pamper-palace resorts could only aspire to.

I smiled my heartfelt thanks. "I'm in search of the Vespa Guardian."

He didn't miss a beat. "Perhaps our new historian can assist you."

"Actually, the vehicle storage area will be just fine." I thanked him and carried Bayle to the Centurion Otis 61 elevator. Originally installed as a steam-operated lift in the 1890s, the wrought-iron cage now ran on electric power. Over the years, it had transported presidents, movie stars, and every reigning Barkview Cavalier. With any luck this ride would be memorable for me, too.

The ornate gate slid open and I greeted the ancient elevator operator. Dressed in starched dark tails and a Victorian striped waistcoat, Will Oldeman was the oldest employee at the hotel. Not to mention the very best informant on the premises. "Hi, Will. This is Bayle."

He acknowledged Bayle with a nod. "My best to Miss Renny."

I smiled. "I'll be sure to tell her." He was a traditionalist to the end; no dog would ever best a Cavalier. "I need to find the Vespa Guardian," I told him. Not a hint of a reaction. "Know where I can find the Vespa?"

"Beach level," he said in a gravelly, chain-smoker kind of

voice as he pushed open the gate. "Be sure to say Mr. Conti sent you."

Code for what, exactly? I'd find out. "Thank you, Will." He'd never led me astray.

Hope stirred as I stepped into what could well be a ship captain's cabin, complete with glistening varnished wood and a model of a sleek nineteenth-century clipper. Leather barrel chairs surrounded glass-topped helm tables. Twin mermaid figureheads framed a beveled mirror above an ornate mahogany bar.

My arm aching, I put Bayle on the ground as I walked through the room to the boardwalk. The fading afternoon sun warmed my face, and fresh salt air filled my senses with instant rightness. I took another deep breath. I was getting closer. I could feel it. Bayle concurred. He sniffed skyward, his steps sure beside me.

Tucked behind the 1950s ice cream parlor, the carriage-style garage door with small panel windows and larger white X panels below opened out, showing off the rental items in a single glance. Beach cruisers, tandem bikes, quadracycles, and razor scooters lined one wall. Surfboards, boogie boards, wetsuits, masks, and fins, in addition to various sand toys, were racked on the other. In between, a lone Segway and fat-tire scooter stood behind a bar-height counter presided over by a stereotypical bleached-blond surfer dude dressed in navy and white board shorts, flip flops and a Barkview Inn logoed tank top.

"Yo. What's hap'nin'?" His hooded eyes barely registered recognition when he flashed me a cowabunga hand wave.

Points for authentic marketing here. No doubt the tourists loved it. "I'm looking for a Vespa."

"Dude?" He scratched his forehead, then gestured toward the wall of bikes and scooters.

"Mr. Conti sent me," I said.

The glazed-over expression vanished. "Gotcha." The surfer dude motioned to another bleached-blond guy in identical attire. He lifted the counter barrier and signaled for me to follow. The sunlit room faded as we walked into a dimly-lit hallway that snaked too many ways, befuddling my directionally-challenged senses. Bayle remained behind me, his eyes watchful.

When we arrived at a metal door protected by a high-tech keypad, the surfer tapped in a code and stepped aside. I entered Barrett-Jackson nirvana. Housed in what looked like an upscale car dealership, a grouping of leather club chairs and a dart board faced a classic Corvette racked above a 2017 Dodge Viper. I recognized Stephan's grandfather's painstakingly-restored 1956 Mercury Monterey "Woody" station wagon in Verona green beside a Harley-Davidson Knucklehead.

Why didn't it surprise me that Barkview had an exclusive car club? No doubt Stephan's grandfather had passed on his membership. Jimmy repaired the vehicles under the strictest secrecy. If not for Will, I'd still be looking for a ghost. How many secrets did idyllic Barkview really have?

"Which vehicle are you picking up?" the surfer asked.

"The Vespa," I said without hesitation.

He directed me toward a shadowed corner. I passed a 1960s racing Ferrari that looked suspiciously like a blockbuster movie prop. Before I could confirm that story, I saw the elusive, classic 1972 black Vespa, a pinkish, half-dollar-size puddle beneath the engine. No surprise, really. I knew who'd killed Howard now. Proving it remained the problem.

CHAPTER 25

"You want to borrow my Jeep to park at the Barkview lookout tonight to make out with me?"

Crammed into the studio control room, sitting ramrod-straight at the call-in switchboard, Sandy's skepticism cracked me up.

"Pretty much. Russ and the chief will stake out the Old Barkview Inn. We'll be in your car at the lookout, just in case our Vespa ghost manages to slip by them." Like that would ever happen. "Russ doesn't want me to be alone." I could do it alone, but karma had brought everyone into place. Truthfully, I hadn't set out to mess up her date with Sean. It just worked out that way.

"Why do you need my Jeep?"

"My car is too recognizable." In retrospect, my personalized KAT4LYF plates hadn't been my best decision. "I need a car the Vespa Guardian would think was a high school kid's."

"You really think the Vespa Guardian will ride tonight?"

"Gabby's spreading a rumor about an after-game meet up. With any luck our ghost will get the message," I said.

"I still don't understand why Russ can't just make an arrest," Sandy said.

With thirty minutes until airtime for my aunt's show, *Throw Him a Bone*, I'd expected more chaos. The poised professional in front of me made me proud. "The evidence is circumstantial," I reminded her. "He's not even confident the DA will prosecute with what we have."

"What world do we live in when having the getaway vehicle, motive, and opportunity isn't good enough?" Sandy voiced my frustration perfectly.

"It's conjecture on the opportunity. We can't identify the actual driver."

"Can't the club folks tell you who checked out the Vespa?" Sandy asked.

"All they will say is that every member has warehouse access. Naturally, there is no security video."

"The joys of a private club."

That even all-knowing Uncle G hadn't known about.

"I'm not so sure I'd call it a club exactly. It's more of a throwback to a long-gone era," I said.

"I can't believe any member can joyride in any other member's car," Sandy said.

"So they say. Apparently, there's a code…"

"Meanwhile, Rayelle will be remanded to federal custody tomorrow."

Sandy's frustration resonated. We had tonight to save her.

"And you get to cook for the Sunday show," Sandy added.

One look at Bayle chasing his red flyball back and forth kick-started my motivation. "At least it isn't a live show." Hives threatened as I contemplated the thought of containing the Tasmanian devil. A horrendous number of takes loomed.

"Do you plan to out the secret car-collecting club?"

"I don't see the point. Tina's grandfather made a deal with

his friend Giuseppe Conti to hide the Vespa until Nonna learned her lesson."

Sandy snickered. "That didn't work out too well. What a macho jerk."

"I agree. Grandpa Principato sounded like a real piece of work."

"So, he created this club?"

"It appears the whole thing just evolved. The fiasco inspired Grandpa McCarthy to restore and stash his cruisin' Woody well out of reach of Grandma McCarthy's Irish temper."

"And so on," Sandy added. "So, how does the Ferrari fit in?"

"Our friendly trash czar won it in a poker game."

"The man who gave up gambling to save his marriage?" Sandy asked.

"Needless to say, Brooke doesn't know," I said.

Sandy's lips pressed together. "You're not going to tell her. Are you?"

Who was I to turn the lives of Brooke and her three children upside down? Maybe Aunt Char had a point about ignorance being bliss. I would never look at him the same way again, but that was my problem.

"Up for the adventure?" I asked.

Sandy exhaled. "Sure. Boring as it will likely be. I'll reschedule with Sean. He'll understand."

With any luck, he wouldn't. Even though I'd cleared him of involvement in Howard's murder, something was still off about him.

CHAPTER 26

Sandy parked in a prime location overlooking Bark Rock. The daytime top lookout view designation did not apply to night-time. Except for the sliver-of-a-sliver moon, the ocean just looked black.

Bayle snored on my lap, his hind legs shaking in puppy dream heaven. I yawned and took another hit of my high-octane Woofing Best coffee in sync with Sandy. Not even a mosquito had buzzed by in the last hour. The fogged windows did prove that we-were-just-talking really could cause the phenomenon.

"Eleven fifty. Doesn't look like the ghost got your message," Sandy said.

"Or Russ and Uncle G caught 'em at the Old Barkview Inn."

"He would've called," Sandy said. "Sean was pretty annoyed I canceled our dinner this afternoon."

I would be too on two hours' notice. "I'm sorry this has been so anticlimactic." I really was. A good story would've gone a long way toward making me feel better about interfering.

I lowered the passenger-side window. Maybe the cool air would keep me awake. If everything went according to plan, Russ and Uncle G should have unveiled the Vespa Guardian. Not that I needed the glory—Rayelle exonerated would be enough. But I'd earned a little action.

Russ's call startled me. "Did you get her?"

"No one in or out. Maybe Gabby's message didn't get out."

Gabby would be crushed. "Did you confirm the Vespa is still inside?"

"Chief is…"

Suddenly, Bayle sprang to all fours and barked like a crazed Doberman. I spun to the right, banging my elbow on the door panel and dropping the phone.

"Cat, what's going on?" His voice faded into the carpet.

Sandy and I saw it then, emerging from the blackness: a filmy, translucent glow forming into a reaperish specter, suspended above ground and angling right for us. Fear paralyzed me. I tried to scream, but gritty dust filled my mouth. This was no ordinary ghost. It called to my darkest fears.

Bayle snapped me out of it. In a white blur, he launched right out the window, banked and turned on his front paws the moment he hit the ground. With flyball efficiency, he flew toward the apparition. In midair, his jaw locked on the edge of the fluttering wisps.

A too-human grunt and a faint but recognizable *rat-ta-ta* sounded as the glowing apparition thumped to the ground and rolled end over end one… two… three times. Bayle held on, shaking his head and growling. Who was this dog, and where had scaredy-Bayle gone?

Distant sirens spurred Sandy and me into action. Sandy turned on the headlights. I grabbed a flashlight and leaped out of the car. Reality hit hard. The black Vespa lay to one side of Sandy's Jeep, the front wheel spinning as I approached. Sure enough, a reflective cape covered the mound. Teeth bared, Bayle, the protector, guarded it.

I motioned Bayle aside. Shockingly, he obeyed as I lifted the cape.

Angela Principato cradled her right arm. "That stupid dog bit me."

No blood. My empathy fizzled. I glanced at Bayle casually licking his paw. "You have bigger problems."

She huffed. "Congratulations, you caught the Vespa Guardian."

"You mean I caught Howard's killer," I said.

She sucked in a breath. "I didn't kill Howard."

I stopped her from reiterating her alibi. "No, you didn't. The alarm was set. You couldn't leave Ciao Bella. The only way out was through the doggie door, which I doubt you could've fit through. The most important clue is..." I shone my light on her ring finger. No ring and no telltale line proving its absence. "You don't wear a wedding ring."

"So? My husband has been dead for five years."

"Nonna does. It's an eternity band, missing one Old World diamond that Bayle found at the murder scene."

Angela's shoulders slumped.

"Was she tracking Howard on Joey's app, or did she just happen to see his location?" I didn't really expect a response from Angela. "The rest was easy. You and Tina always made the limoncello on Sunday night. So Nonna had time before Tina took the children home. She put on her reflective dog-walking sweat suit and crawled through Bolt's doggie door, then walked to the Old Barkview Inn and retrieved the Vespa. She drove to Bichon Bisquets, stashed the Vespa behind the lilac planter, and snuck into the barkery. She didn't intend to kill Howard. I'm guessing she confronted Howard about leaving Tina and he dismissed her, just as her husband had done to her years ago. In anger, she grabbed the nearest thing, which happened to be Rayelle's Bichon knife, and threw it at Howard."

No comment needed from Angela. I'd gotten it right. I could tell. The sirens were almost upon us, the flashing lights brightening the road.

"I do have a question. How did you find out about the Vespa?" I asked.

"My husband and father were kindred souls. He passed the Vespa to my husband. When he died, Mr. Conti, old goat that he was, came to me."

"I thought it was a good-old-boys club."

"Oh, it was. My husband left it to my eldest son, who deeded it to me. Help me up. I'm getting too old for this." Sandy and I helped her stand, bearing most of her weight as her arthritic knees groaned in protest.

"Why did Nonna do it? Howard broke his family tradition to become an inventor. He would have accepted Joey's dreams."

Angela exhaled. "Howard bringing Rayelle to town pushed Nonna over the top. She thought Tina had ended up in the same destructive relationship we'd both had."

"He wanted Bayle on his flyball team," I said.

Angela shrugged. "My mother didn't see it that way. She saw a man exactly like my father and the man I married destined to ruin Tina's life. While my mother failed to protect me, she was determined to protect her granddaughter." I heard the catch in Angela's voice as Russ and Uncle G arrived, sirens blaring. Bayle retreated behind my legs.

"Are you all right?" Russ asked.

I nodded before returning my full attention to Angela. "Nonna sacrificed herself for Tina?"

"Nonna has brain cancer. The doctors say she has less than six months."

Talk about sucking the air right out of us all. Russ and I shared a glance. Nonna would never go to trial. What a mess. Tina had lost a good husband and Joey and Bianca a father. The world had lost a gifted inventor. For what? Fear of repeating mistakes.

Tina and the children would find some way to go on. Howard would never see his children grow up, but Tina and Aunt Char would see to it they knew of Howard's sacrifice.

At least Rayelle would be released. Don't ask me how, but somehow Bayle knew. He practically corralled Russ and I and herded us toward Russ's car. I didn't have the heart to tell him nothing could happen until the morning.

CHAPTER 27

Reuniting Bayle and Rayelle should've been the highlight of my week. Four days dealing with a high-maintenance, anxiety-prone dog with obedience issues should've been enough for a lifetime. And it was. At least I told myself that as I stood outside police headquarters waiting for Rayelle's release. Why, then, did I feel so empty?

Bayle paced beside me, his eyes never leaving the glass doors. How he knew what was going on I couldn't begin to guess. I just accepted it as I did the communication between my aunt and Renny.

Russ texted me a moment before he opened the door and escorted Rayelle outside. Bayle ripped the leash right out of my hand, flyball-flew fifty feet, and leaped into Rayelle's outstretched arms. His paws around her neck, they twirled in a joyous reunion. Tears threatened. To be loved like that.

I acknowledged Rayelle's thank-you with a nod and turned to go. I knew that she'd call me after a water-wasting shower for details. Now was her time with Bayle. I got it.

Russ would be staying on in Barkview, at least for a while,

which meant whatever Howard had started with the medical implants for diabetics remained active. Much as I wanted to know the truth, protecting Aunt Char and Sandy came first. Nothing like defining priorities in your life.

Bayle's bark stopped me cold. Something was wrong. I turned in time to catch Bayle as he leaped into my arms. His front paws wrapped around my neck, his heart pressed against mine as he licked my cheek, then he wiggled out of my arms and returned to Rayelle, his tail wagging in bliss.

His silly antics made me smile. I couldn't help myself.

Russ's whisper tickled my ear. "They manage to work their way into your heart."

Who'd have guessed? Bayle drove me crazy, but I was going to miss his warmth and enthusiasm. He really did make me laugh. Sure, I'd see him often, but his first loyalty was to Rayelle.

Was I ready for that kind of commitment of my own?

I thought about the charm bracelet Ariana had given me. Maybe my dog fostering was a journey. If I listed the advantages and disadvantages of a Cavalier King Charles Spaniel and a Bichon Frise, would either breed win? There were hundreds of dog breeds and mixes. Perhaps there was a perfect dog for me.

I turned in Russ's embrace and looked into his promising blue eyes. "Come on. Let's go home."

The End

Join Cat on her quest for the perfect dog when she teams up with a German Shepherd to locate a stolen diamond and avenge the murder of an Olympic defector in *Shepherded to Death*.

Hope you enjoyed your adventure in the dog-friendliest place in America. To learn more about Barkview and Cat's next adventure visit: www.cbwilsonauthor.com.

Sign up for **The Bark View** a monthly update all things Barkview including:

* *Friday Funnies*, pet related cartoons
* Recipes from *Bichon Bisquets Barkery's* canine kitchen
* Cool merchandise ideas from the *Bow Wow Boutique*.
* Not to mention Barkview news and fun contests.

Don't miss Cat's next adventure:

Available Now: Shepherded to Death

A stolen diamond, a murdered jewel thief and a sabotaged pickleball tournament can't possibly have anything in common. But, every event leads back to newly-elected Mayor Charlotte Barklay's Founders' Day celebration. Who would want to sabotage a Barkview tradition?

Cat Wright can think of a few folks, including the former mayor. When the evidence leads Cat to a colorful gypsy fortune teller and prophecy portends events; Cat can't help but wonder if a real king is hiding in this quaint seaside community.

Can Cat and her German Shepherd partner protect their pack from secrets that could change history as we know it?

Get your copy of Shepherded to Death today!

ACKNOWLEDGMENTS

To my writing cheerleaders, who endlessly listened to my ideas, edit my spelling and grammar, help research and recipe test, thank you Pam Wright, Dee Kaler, and Brandi Wilson.

For research and police procedure assistance, thank you Richard R. Zitzke, Chief of Police, Whitehall, Ohio, retired. I assure you any errors are entirely my fault.

Thank you Donna Templin for my adventures with Katie. She's the star of the show.

ABOUT THE AUTHOR

Award-winning author C.B. Wilson's love of writing was spurred by an early childhood encounter with a Nancy Drew book where she wrote what she felt was a better ending. The Barkview Mysteries combine C. B.'s love of mysteries and dogs. The current ten book series follows Cat Wright, a feline-loving, former investigative reporter's, journey to find the right dog for her. An animal lover, C.B.'s motivation to grow this popular series is a result of her belief that every animal deserves a forever home. You will likely find adoptable dogs at her appearances.

A graduate of the Gemological Institute of America, C.B. enjoys sharing her passion for discovering lost, stolen and missing gems in her stories. Her best plots seem to come while on horseback in the Arizona desert. She is an avid pickleball player and admits to being a true chocoholic.

Join C.B. in Barkview and help Cat decide if there is a perfect dog for our resident cat lover.

To connect with C.B Wilson:
www.cbwilsonauthor.com
www.facebook.com/cbwilsonauthor
instagram.com/cbwilsonauthor